I'M STILL
ELODY ELIZABETH

Molly McNamara Carter

For Rhye

Text copyright © 2024 by Molly Carter
Cover Illustrations copyright © 2024 by Shahrzad Salehi

Published by Lawley Publishing,
a division of Lawley Enterprises LLC.
All rights reserved.

No part of this publication may be reproduced, or stored in a retrieval system, or transmitted in any form or by any means, electronic, mechanical, photocopying, recording, or otherwise, without written permission of the publisher.

This book is a work of fiction. Any reference to historical events, real people, or real locales are used as fiction in the work. Other names, characters, places and incidents are all a product of the author's imagination and any resemblance to actual events, locales or people, living or dead is purely coincidental.

Hardcover ISBN 978-1-960137-56-2
Paperback ISBN 978-1-960137-58-6
Library of Congress Number: 2023952364

For information regarding permissions, write to:
Lawley Publishing
Attention: Permissions Department
70 S Val Vista Drive #A3 #188
Gilbert, AZ 85296
LawleyPublishing.com

CONTENTS

Alliteration	1
One Hundred Weeks	2
The Thing	4
Except for the Ones on the Page	5
The Really Huge Problem	9
Swoon	11
My People	14
It's a Little Crazy	16
Blue Like the Sky on a Summer's Day	18
The Intricate Flavors of Instant Ramen	26
The Star That Will Take It to Her	29
Gotta Take What I Can Get	31
On His Team	33
Up and Down the Keys	40
Smashing My Dreams	47
Puckered Against My Pillow	50
The Same Gene Pool	55
Frank Sinatra	60
One Song, One Assignment, One Hour	63

Modern-Day Beethoven	70
That. Was. Not. The. Real. Me.	73
The Solution to World Hunger	78
Over Before it Began	81
Putrid Smell Of Dog Poop	84
Like Cockroaches From the Light	89
A Mingle of Depressing Notes	92
Strangely Just as Comforting	95
All About That Bass	98
Butterflies Having a Dance-Off	102
Now We're Both Blushing	108
One Three-Letter Word	112
Very Socially Inept	113
A Very Squishy Flower Garden	119
Nice Kitty Cats	125
Like the Dam Broke	130
My Leg as a Peeing Pole	136
On a Cool Autumn Breeze	141
I'm Still Elody Elizabeth	147
Hugs That Feel Like Home	149

Swimming in a Pool Full of Notes	153
Mistaken for Raisin Prints	159
Not Sunday!	163
This Is Who I Am	166
So Not Okay	171
At This Time Tomorrow	175
Light Halos Behind His Head	177
Slightly More Awkward	182
A Tiny Waste of My, Well, Life	186
Nearly Kissing Him in the Process	188
Face-Splitting Grin	195
Maybe It Isn't Zane	199
Never Felt So Good	202
Always Be My El Belle	205

CHAPTER ONE

ALLITERATION

My name is Elody Elizabeth. Since I was little, people have confused my name with Melody. Because, well, that makes sense since Melody is a real name. But no, my name is Elody. Like a beautiful song without the "M." My mom said she liked the alliteration of Elody Elizabeth. So basically, I got to learn what the word alliteration meant at a very young age and have spent a lifetime (and by lifetime, I mean all 13 years of my life) correcting people.

CHAPTER TWO

ONE HUNDRED WEEKS

There's a boy who lives down the street named Zane. I've been in love with him for one hundred years. Seriously. Okay, fine, maybe not one hundred years, seeing that I'm only 13, but at least one hundred weeks, for sure.

He's my neighbor and, like I said, lives down the street from us. I've watched him drive by with his older brother every school day for the last 47 school days since his brother got his license and they quit taking the bus. It sounds a little stalker-ish now that I'm saying it, but it's not like I follow him around or anything. My bedroom window is at the front of the house, and our house sits at a strange angle facing the street, so if I look out my window (which also happens to be next to my mirror), I can see the entire street from my house to, you guessed it, his house. And if I happen to be at my window, I mean my mirror, and happen to glance out the window at exactly 8:17 every weekday morning (except Thursday, which is his late-start day), I'll probably see him getting into his car and driving past my house.

Zane's a grade older than me, a freshman in high school, and you'd think I'd at least talk to him, but I haven't, and I don't because, well, there's this thing.

CHAPTER THREE
THE THING

Here's the thing. I'm shy, like petrifyingly shy. Like I should be the poster child for introverts. Like I have JOMO (Joy-of-Missing-Out) instead of FOMO (Fear-of-Missing-Out). Like my face turns bright red if the wrong person even looks at me too long, or at all. Raising my hand in class? No way. Talking to strangers? Not a chance. Performing in public? In your dreams! Or more like nightmares. You'd think I was going to perform a solo in Abravanel Hall for the nerves that wrack my body.

Chapter Four

EXCEPT FOR THE ONES ON THE PAGE

You see, there was an "incident." Once (two years ago, but I'm still trying to get over it, so it feels like yesterday, and I refer to the "incident" like it was yesterday), I performed a piano piece at a talent show for school. It was the most embarrassing moment OF MY LIFE. I couldn't breathe for the twenty minutes while I waited for my turn, looking down at the program every other second to see how much closer my name was. Then, when it was my turn, I walked to the piano on wobbly legs, sweat practically spewing from my armpits. I sat at the piano, looking at the music, then I began to hit the keys with my fingers. I would say, "play" the keys or notes, but there wasn't much of that. My hands were shaking so badly that I hit every note on the piano except for the ones that were actually written on the page.

Here's the other thing—I'm actually a pretty

great pianist. I can admit it because I'm not that great at a lot of things, but with piano, I don't have to talk to anyone, so I practice a lot. My piano teachers have never had to bribe me to practice like they did my sister. My parents finally gave up on her. Mom always says I got my musical abilities from my dad's side, that and my height, too. Yep. I'm short. Like really short. I mean, I'm not like a small person if that's what you're thinking, just always the smallest person in any group. Always. I hated lining up by height when I was in elementary school. It always felt like there was this spotlight on me, and everyone would turn to look at me.

When I was little, my dad signed me up for soccer. He thought it might help with my coordination and increase my athletic abilities (P.S. He was wrong). On the first day of practice, they handed out jerseys and, of course, had us line up by height. I was a full—adult—head shorter than the next kid, and sure enough, my jersey was like a dress on me. Let's just say we quickly realized soccer was never going to be my thing. I fantasize about being average height, stuck right in the middle between girls named Maddison and Sydney . . .

I digress (a cool word I learned from a book) . . . back to the talent show. So, not only did I hit every note except for what was written because my hands were shaking, but my legs were shaking, too. My foot that was supposed to be on the pedal kept jumping around, making my knee hit the bottom side of the piano, creating this strange thump every few measures that didn't match any beat or rhythm of the song. When "it" (I'm not even sure what to call it because it wasn't really a song or piece of music) was over, everyone looked at each other and clapped because what else were they supposed to do? I walked/ran straight out the back door and called my mom to come pick me up. I had forgotten that she was out of town, and since I couldn't remember my dad's number, I told the lady at the office that I didn't feel well. I spent the rest of the day lying in the nurse's office with an ice pack on my head. Honestly, I can't even remember what I said to convince her that I couldn't go back to class, but it worked.

    That was the important thing. For a full two hours, I could close my eyes and pretend that the world couldn't see me since I couldn't see them. Like when little kids play peekaboo and think you really disappear when they can't see you. Needless to say, I haven't done a talent show since. In fact, I've refused to even participate in my piano teacher's recitals. She doesn't quite understand, being that, as I said before, I'm a pretty great pianist, but she goes along with it because that was the deal when I started training with her after the talent show incident and, well, my dad pays the bill so I win.

CHAPTER FIVE
THE REALLY HUGE PROBLEM

But there is a problem. A huge problem, really. You see, my piano teacher, Mrs. Cleary, keeps hinting that I've progressed beyond what she can teach. She is not very subtle about this, and sometimes I wonder if I'm doing a good job of ignoring her hints or if she is trying to be nice by not kicking me off her list. She keeps tucking fliers in my theory book about music schools, music academies, and professional instructors who have little blurbs next to their faces, *"Now accepting new student applications."* I've looked at their websites. I'm not that oblivious to what she is trying to do. They look amazing; some have a perfect mix of pop and classical music, plus flexible times, and Dad is committed to this. He tells me that the tuition is a fraction of what I'm worth (I love it when Dad says things like that), plus, if I'm serious about pursuing music in college, I need this kind of training and experience. But here's the big problem: All of them require an audition recording. I've tried to get up the courage, but every time I set it up, I end up stumbling along so badly I might as well have been playing chopsticks. My dad finally quit asking me if I wanted to record. I think it had begun stressing him out as much as it was me. So, I continue to work with the piano teacher I have and keep putting off any decisions.

Chapter Six

SWOON

Okay, now, where were we? Oh yes, I was talking about Zane. Long pause here for a proper swoon. Have you ever looked up the word *swoon*? I love looking up old-fashioned words I find in books that we never use anymore. Swoon literally means "Faint from extreme emotion." My mom loves old movies where the heroine puts the back of her hand to her forehead before collapsing. That may be what you think of when you think of the word *swoon*. I think of it more of me sitting at my window, I mean mirror, with my head resting on my arms, watching for Zane to drive by. Swoon.

Wow, get on track, Elody!

Where was I? Oh yes! Zane, the boy down the street who has been the king of my crush castle for the last hundred weeks. Have I mentioned that not only do I see him drive to school each day, but every once in a while, I see him play basketball next door with Dean? Dean lives next door. He's always been like this big brother/best friend to me. He's a grade older than me like Zane is, and Dean and I have been friends since my family moved here when I was six. His house has this huge yard and basketball court, and lots of kids from the neighborhood come and play on it. Once in a while, Zane comes over to Dean's house, and they shoot hoops. Dean is actually really good, probably better than Zane, but Zane hit his growth spurt first, so he has height on his side.

Sometimes, when I'm over at Dean's, I'll watch him shoot hoops while I do homework on the grass of our adjoining yards. He used to ask me to play with him, but it's ridiculous. It wouldn't matter if I miraculously became good at basketball; he is so much taller than I am that it would take very little effort for him to reach up and grab any ball I attempted to shoot. I like watching Dean play because he talks to me while shooting and tells me about his day, school, or whatever else is going on. He's a good talker, you know, the kind of person that you can hang out with and not say much but feel like you just had a whole conversation because they pretty much carried it. Those are the best kind of friends for people like me who'd rather not talk too much, or much at all. But to be honest, sometimes when Dean is shooting and talking, and I'm lying on the grass trying to read or finish homework, I just say, "uh-huh" every minute or so just to make him think I'm still listening, when really I have no idea what he's saying. But what do you do? He's my best friend, and he talks a lot. I mean A LOT.

Dean used to have a crush on my older sister, Violet. He would ask about her all the time and ask me to go invite her to hang out with us. Finally, when she graduated from high school, he clued in and realized she would never be into him. (Earth to Dean, she is WAY older than you!) I acted like I didn't know because it was so annoying. I'd walk inside and count to 60 twice (never 120; that's not nearly as fun), then come outside and say she was busy. I liked to make up weird things that she was doing, like "cutting her toenails," "washing her curtains," or "practicing tongue twisters," just to see if Dean ever caught on. He didn't. I know how this makes him sound, but, believe it or not, he is actually really smart, just not so smart in the girl department.

Chapter Seven
MY PEOPLE

Violet got married last summer. She was only 20, and Dad thought she was too young, but Mom said girls in her family married young and stayed married, so who cares? (Even though she was the exception to the getting married young thing . . . she and Dad are still married.) Mom is like that, different from everyone else's moms. She sees the world differently than most parents. She just goes with the flow of whatever is happening. Her parents always called her their Hippie Girl. She's a traveling journalist and has traveled my entire life. Violet and I had a nanny when we were young because Dad owns his own company and occasionally used to travel with Mom. Sometimes, Mom will be home for weeks at a time, and we get to do all sorts of interesting projects like repaint my bedroom, plant rose bushes, or make hundreds of hygiene kits for the homeless. Mom is like that, super creative and always has to be doing something. Then, she will be gone again, and Dad and I slow down and get into a kind of boring but comfortable routine before Mom comes home again and almost wakes us up. It would probably be a little crazy for most people, but we aren't most people. They are my people, and it all kind of works for us.

CHAPTER EIGHT
IT'S A LITTLE CRAZY

Did I mention that I don't go to school anymore? You're probably wondering how I can happen to be at my mirror (fine, window) when I, too, should be driving to school. It's not like I dropped out or just quit. I'm homeschooled. I went until two years ago (right after the talent show incident, but unrelated, I promise). After my older sister Violet graduated, Mom decided she wanted to have the flexibility for me to travel with her sometimes when she does, so she pulled me out. It's a little crazy sometimes, but I like it. At first, it was weird not having a real schedule, but I got used to that fast. I do most of my work online, except for piano lessons, and once in a while, I have a tutor if there is something I'm studying that turns out to be a little too complicated. Dad does most of his work from home, so it doesn't get too lonely. In the first few months, I went on a couple of trips with Mom, but I soon realized I liked being home more. So I don't travel with her so much anymore, but I decided I like doing school from home. It kind of just works for me.

Chapter Nine

BLUE LIKE THE SKY ON A SUMMER'S DAY

In the afternoons, when I hear the thud-swish of the basketball hoop, I know Dean is home, and I gather up my notebook and whatever else I need and go outside. Dean loves to give me the lowdown after school each day, all the drama of high school life, which seems much more interesting than the drama of two years ago when I quit going to school. I'm usually done with everything, but if not, I take my homework with me, and we meet at the basketball hoop. He gets his "sitting-too-long-engery" out shooting hoops, and I sit and listen. Sometimes, I write love poems to Zane. Of course, I don't give them to him; they stay in my love poem notebook (that conveniently looks like a regular notebook, so if I'm writing in front of Dean, he doesn't know).

"Hey, Elody!" he calls as soon as the door is shut, which means he's been watching for me. It's Friday, and he probably has something he thinks is juicy to share from the school week.

"Hey, Dean," I call back as I walk across the lawn toward him. I sit down in the shade with my back against the tree and open up my notebook, even though I know we'll be talking. "How was school today?"

"It was good. Nothing new." I watch him for a few minutes, confused. I know he's lying. He keeps missing his shots, and Dean hardly ever misses. But for some reason, he has something to tell me, and he's having a hard time saying it.

"Nothing?" I ask, hoping to prompt him.

Dribble, dribble, thunk. Again, no swish.

"Nah, not really,"

I shrug and turn my attention to my notebook. But after a few minutes of unusual silence, I glance back up and see that Dean is watching me.

"What?"

"Nothing, I was just wondering what you're writing about."

"Homework," I answer too fast and slam the notebook closed. "Just a project for my English class," I tell him, trying to recover casually.

"What is it?" Dean stops dribbling and carries the ball over to me, plopping down next to me on the grass. He never does this, and my heart begins to pound. He is way too close to my love poem book.

"Oh, it's a poetry project. You wouldn't like it."

"Try me."

He brushes his dark curls out of his eyes and looks straight at me. I feel like his brown eyes are seeing through the cover of my notebook. My heart pounds faster, and I scramble in my head, trying to think of something, anything to distract him.

"So, it's about this um, place in uh . . ."

Ironically, I'm saved by the one person who makes my heart pound faster than the thought of Dean reading my love poem book.

"Dean, you shooting hoops?"

Zane.

Both Dean and I look up at the same time to see Zane standing on the other side of the driveway with his basketball underneath his arm, a look of confusion on his face.

"Hey, Zane. Yeah, I am. Want to play one-on-one?" Dean jumps up without a word to me, and I let out a sigh of relief.

I open up the notebook and pretend to be totally absorbed by the words on the page as I listen to Zane and Dean.

"What were you doing?" Zane asks Dean as if I'm not still sitting right here.

"Oh, Elody was just going to tell me about a poem she's been working on for school." He says this casually while dribbling between his legs and sinking a shot. Whatever was on his mind before is gone now.

"You like poetry now, Dean?" Zane asks. I'm watching them, not because I'm worried about Dean's response, but because I can see Zane trying to get into Dean's head, trying to steal the ball from him.

"Only if your mom writes it," Dean says and moves around Zane so fast Zane has to spin with barely enough time to see Dean sink a perfect layup.

I know a perfect layup when I see one because I have watched Dean for too many years trying to perfect his. And when he fails, you can see it all over his face. But right now, his face is split into the biggest grin in the history of grins. You'd think he'd won the lottery.

"That's two, take it back behind the line," Dean says, motioning to the back of the driveway. Zane rolls his eyes.

"Eh, just you wait. I'm coming for you." But he isn't, and Dean snags the ball from him before he's even close to the net.

Even though I should be cheering for Dean, the truth is, I don't care who wins or who has the best layup. I just can't believe my luck. Zane usually doesn't come over when I'm here with Dean. I wait for every opportunity to see Zane, and here he is in front of me. I try to casually watch them play, pretending that I don't care about either of them.

Before long, another boy in the neighborhood shows up. He's younger than all of us but is always up for anything. He wants to play, but Dean tells him he can't because he'll make the teams uneven.

"What if she plays?" Zane says to Dean, motioning to me as if I can't hear him.

"Elody? Elody doesn't play basketball." The disbelief on Dean's face hurts something deep inside of me that I don't understand, but I don't have time to figure it out.

"Oh, come on, let's ask her." Zane turns toward me and walks across the driveway and onto the grassy lawn that separates mine and Dean's house. I pretend I hadn't heard anything and move my pen across an almost blank page.

"Hey, wanna play?"

Remember how I said that I'd been in love with him for a hundred weeks? Did I also mention that we'd never actually ever spoken to each other? I mean, you'd think we would have since we've grown up down the road from each other, but nope. Not a single word since we were little kids, and obviously, I don't remember anything we could have said then. I look up, and there he is, crouching down in front of me, ball poised between his fingertips. His eyes are much bluer than I realized, seeing them this close. Blue like the sky on a summer's day. I think what a great line that would be for one of my poems, and I can feel my face flush with embarrassment, and a tiny irritation tickles inside of me. Why does my body always betray me at the worst moments? Dad always says that my inner feelings are so strong that they spill over onto my outer expressions. I think that's his nice way of saying I blush easily.

"Uh, me?" I mumble.

"Yeah, you can be on Dean's team to balance him out since he thinks he's such hot stuff."

"I don't know how to play," I say, even though that's kind of a lie. I may not have ever really tried to play before, like really play, but I know how. Between my dad watching every college game he can and the innumerable days I've sat here watching Dean, I *know* how. I just haven't ever tried. I mean, I've tried to shoot hoops, but I've never actually tried to play a game, be on a team, dribble around the court. But having the knowledge and being able to actually execute are two completely different things, but at this moment, I definitely don't have the verbal abilities to explain that to Zane.

"That's okay, we'll teach you," Zane says.

He bounces a little on his feet, still in the crouching position, waiting for me.

"Zane, leave her alone. She doesn't want to play," Dean calls over to him, but Zane ignores him and flashes me the smile I've seen in every edition of the yearbook since I convinced Dad to let me start buying them in third grade.

"Come on, we need you." He has never spoken two words to me, and now he needs me. As if in a trance induced by the power of his smile, I set my notebook on the grass next to the tree trunk and stand up. Zane turns to Dean triumphantly. "See, she's cool. Now the teams are even." But the look on Dean's face seems more concerned than relieved that there are now even teams, and I feel a strange confusion in the back of my head. But I don't have time to figure that out either. The words are running through my head, like a tacky neon Vegas sign repeatedly flashing Zane's words, "She's Cool."

I stand on the court catty-corner to the net. Zane passes the ball to the little neighbor kid, who dribbles and passes back right to Zane, who has run up and is now under the net. Side-stepping Dean, he catches the pass and makes a layup. Dean catches the ball as I stand in confusion, still in a trance, when Dean's phone beeps. He pulls it out and says, "Sorry, guys, dinner's ready. I gotta go." He glances toward me with a look of apology in his eyes. Then, he dribbles right into the garage.

"See ya tomorrow!" Zane calls after him. Then he and the neighbor kid dribble their balls right down the road toward his house. It takes me a second to realize I'm still standing in Dean's driveway. Exactly where I was when the game started. My first and only basketball game over before it really even began. There's a strange sense of relief like I don't have to make a fool of myself, and yet there's also a little disappointment. Here I was for the first time actually in a game with Zane. And now it's over.

Chapter Ten

THE INTRICATE FLAVORS OF INSTANT RAMEN

I pick up my things next to the tree and go inside. Dad is still working. We're not big all-sit-around-the-dinner-table people; in fact, since Violet left, we pretty much only eat at the table on weekends if Mom is home. I usually make whatever is easy (meaning within minutes and in the microwave) and eat it at the bar in the kitchen, and Dad, who usually works late, eats in front of the TV.

Violet is an excellent cook. It was kind of her thing. When she quit piano, Mom said she had to choose something as a hobby, and she decided it was cooking. She was so good, in fact, that she won a scholarship to a culinary arts school while she was still in high school. After she graduated, she got a job at this amazing restaurant in Park City, where we got to eat when we went and visited her. Every portion was the size of a quarter, but still really good. And since she is one of their chefs, we got to try everything. Good thing we did, or we would have been starving afterward.

The problem is that because Violet always made us these amazing meals, I never learned how to make anything. Dad doesn't seem to mind much, though. I make some instant ramen and am just sitting down when my phone beeps. I don't have many people who text me. Mom, of course, when she's away, Violet, and Dean. I pick it up.

DEAN:	Hey, sorry. Mom had dinner, and I was late. You know how she gets about dinner.
ME:	It's okay. Say hi for me.
DEAN:	She says I should have invited you over.
ME:	Then I'd have missed out on the intricate flavors of instant ramen.
DEAN:	Yeah, wouldn't want to miss that . . .
DEAN:	Hey, sorry about that earlier.
ME:	About what?
DEAN:	You know, the whole making you play thing.
ME:	It's okay, it wasn't you.
DEAN:	Sorry anyway.
DEAN:	Oh, GTG

I set the phone down and blow at a forkful of steaming ramen. The apology confuses me. Why does Dean feel bad about Zane asking me to play? He said

I was cool! Now that my mind is back on Dean, what did he want to tell me?

CHAPTER ELEVEN
THE STAR THAT WILL TAKE IT TO HER

I'm sitting on my bed writing a love poem about Zane, wondering what it would sound like with a melody, when my phone pings again.

VIOLET: Hey! How was your day?
ME: Good. Nothing new.
VIOLET: Have you talked to Mom yet tonight?
ME: No. Not yet, why?
VIOLET: Hmmmm . . . just curious.

Immediately, I pull up Mom's number on my favorites and hit call. It rings, but no answer. Then I text.

ME: Hey Mom! Just calling to say goodnight.

Nothing. I look out the window, then add another line to my poem.

Today, you told me I was cool.
Do I believe you, or am I just a fool?

Dad sticks his head into my room and says goodnight. No response from Mom. Sometimes it's like that. She's always in different time zones and can't always talk. It's okay, though. I move my gaze out the window from Zane's house up to the stars. Mom always says that if we can't talk, say goodnight to the stars, and they will take it to her.

"Goodnight, Mom," I say to the brightest one I can see. I know it's probably a planet, but I like to pretend it's the star that takes my "goodnight" to Mom.

CHAPTER TWELVE

GOTTA TAKE WHAT I CAN GET

Today is a new day, a new start. After breakfast, I practice the piano. My teacher, Mrs. Cleary, always reminds me to set an alarm, not so I practice enough, but so I stop practicing. She is sure that because I pass off each new piece so quickly, I must get nothing else done in my life. She is also sure that I'll never really improve without stretching myself, and she does not mean trying to reach further on the keyboard.

But today, I am more distracted than I normally am. I still have unanswered questions about what Dean was hiding and what Violet was talking about, but questions or no questions, I've got things to do, and I'm moving down my list. And on my list is to write a new love poem. Today's poem is all about Zane's smile. This is not the first love poem I've written to him about his smile. In fact, it's a topic that seems to come up an awful lot. Sometimes, I lay all the yearbooks out on my bed, open the page with his face on it, and compare them. You can almost see him change as he gets older. Each year, his smile gets a little bigger until the last couple, you can see he's perfected that little extra pull on the right side. His signature breath-taking, heart-pounding, swoon-worthy smile. I know this sounds a little stalker-ish, too, but I don't tell him that I do this, and hey, I look at pictures of Dean and other people I know as well.

When I first started homeschooling, I asked Mom if I could have a social media account. I gave her a list of all the social benefits that I could possibly come up with, ways I could stay in touch with friends from school since I wouldn't be seeing them on a daily basis (yeah, it's not like I had that many, but I was willing to use whatever I had to get SM). I could stay informed about activities that were happening in the school and locally so I could attend (like I'd ever, or had ever!) and even be able to follow news and global events (really?). It didn't matter, though; even with all my pleading and a well-prepared case, Mom said no. I mean, maybe she sees the stalker-ish obsessive personality I have and was wise, or maybe she wants to make my life miserable. Could be either one. But the fact is, while other people scroll social media and look at pictures of their crushes, I'm stuck with old-fashioned yearbooks, so I gotta take what I can get.

Chapter Thirteen

ON HIS TEAM

When I hear Dean's thunk and swish, my heart begins to pound in anticipation, and I put sneakers on before going out to meet him. I still bring a notebook (not the love poem one; that was a little too close call yesterday), but I'm hoping that I won't be using it. Zane had clearly said, "See you tomorrow," and today is tomorrow. I pause a few minutes by the door, waiting to see if I hear any more balls being dribbled, and then I give up and go outside anyway. It's only Dean outside, and a look of relief passes over his face when he sees me come outside.

"Hey, Elody!" he says.

"Hey, Dean," I say and take my place against the tree like always. I open the notebook but can't focus; anticipation is eating me alive. I keep glancing up the road, waiting to see if Zane is coming. Dean is talking like always, but when I glance up, he's not dribbling.

He's standing there with his ball under one arm and a weird look on his face.

"What?" I ask.

"Elody, I asked you a question," he says slowly, like something is wrong with me. And something is. I glance away from Dean and see Zane jogging down the road, bouncing his ball to match his giant steps.

"You did? What question?" I say, trying to get my focus back on Dean.

"I asked you what you did today," he says again as if I'm hard of hearing.

"Today?" I can't help it; my eyes have a mind of their own and are back watching Zane's sandy blonde hair as the front flops, matching each bounce of the ball as he dribbles down the sidewalk in giant steps. I peel my eyes off him and turn back to Dean, but not before Dean turns to see what had my attention.

He sighs, "Never mind," and turns to shoot a perfect three-pointer.

I don't have time to respond before Zane calls out to Dean, and they immediately begin a competitive game of one-on-one. Instead of saying anything, I bury myself in my notebook. It takes me a solid ten minutes to realize that instead of grabbing the notebook with my history notes in it, I'd grabbed an old notebook from math—two years ago. I pretend to be reading anyway, occasionally underlining

On His Team

random answers, making squiggles near the top of the page as if I'm making notes to myself. I try not to keep glancing up, but one time, when I do, I catch Zane's eye, and he smiles at me. That same smile I'd been writing about from my room this morning. The butterflies in my stomach are short-lived as the minutes tick by, and neither of them invites me to play. It's not that I suddenly have a burning desire to play basketball. I mean, I'm still as short as I ever was, but I want Zane to want me to play so badly that I feel like I'll explode if he doesn't invite me. I know the time is ticking closer to Dean's dinner text from his mom. I am almost panicking when the little neighbor boy shows up.

"Guys, can I play?" he asks.

"Only if she does," Zane replies with a smile and a nod toward me.

"Her name is Elody," Dean replies, impatience in his voice. Before he can say that I don't play or don't want to, I stand up.

"I'll play." I'm even surprising myself at this point. I mean, I purposely put my sneakers on, but still, who do I think I am? That I somehow became an NBA all-star overnight? Or have any experience playing basketball at all? I am clear about one thing in life. I am a klutz. I'm pretty sure I've already made that clear, so now basketball?

"Elody, you don't have to," Dean says through his teeth as he moves closer to me.

"It's fine, I can play," I respond, suddenly annoyed at Dean. Why is he so adamant that I don't play?

"Yeah, there we go!" Zane says enthusiastically. "You can be on my team this time." At this point, I pretty much melt. MAJOR SWOON. I mean, first, he acknowledged me. Then, he called me cool, and now, today, the king of my crush castle wants me on his team? Who cares if it's basketball or not? He wants me on his team! Zane is coming toward me with the ball under one arm, with the other arm raised for a high five. I feel like I'm soaring and reach up to smack his hand. I guess playing the piano doesn't increase your hand-eye coordination because the "five" lands off-centered and is more like a two, with my smallest fingers the only ones to make contact with his hand. Zane's eyebrows join together in confusion, and then he shrugs.

"Okay, well, that works too," Zane laughs and dribbles the ball to the back of the driveway, ready to pass it in. I've been in the game for two seconds. Two seconds! And have already shown my incredible lack of athletic ability. As he's dribbling, watching me for an empty space around Dean to pass the ball in, I begin to wonder if this is a good idea. I mean, if I can't complete a successful high five, how am I supposed to play basketball? Then the ball is coming toward me. And my incredible reflex skills kick in. Just not the reflex skills I was hoping for. You know, the ones you actually use for things like, say, basketball. Instead of reaching out to catch the ball, I throw my hands over my face to protect myself, crouch down, and scream. Yep, that's right. I scream because a basketball is being passed to me. And honestly, at that moment, it seems to be coming rather fast. But the ball doesn't hit me. Instead, it bounces next to me, then slows to a roll as it goes down the driveway and into the road. I look up from my crouching position to see everyone standing there with their jaws dropped, trying to figure out what just happened. I can't make eye contact. I feel my hands start to shake, and I jump up and run.

I obviously don't even wait to see anyone's reaction. Grabbing my notebook, I run full speed (which, let's be honest, isn't that fast) across the yard and into my house. I slam the door shut and lean against it as if keeping the horrible incident from following me. Then, it all hits me. My crush, the boy I've been in love with for a hundred weeks, is outside, inviting me to be on his team, and THAT was what happened. Slowly, I slump to the floor, hide my head on my knees, and the tears begin to flow.

The doorbell rings, jolting my tears to silence. I know it's Dean, but I don't answer. I can hear him on the other side of the door, calling my name, but I ignore him. Even after he rings the doorbell three times. He finally leaves, and I resume my cry. Dad must have heard the doorbell (I mean, he obviously heard the doorbell) and comes out. One look at me, and instead of saying anything, he sits down next to me, leaning against the door, and wraps his arm around me, pulling me close. That's the thing about my dad; he doesn't make a big deal about anything. He doesn't even say much either, but when it counts, he's there. As he wraps his arm around me, I lean into him, and we sit like that until the tears stop, and the gulps stop, and I hear my stomach rumble. He lifts my chin so I have to look at him straight in the eye, and just when I think he's going to give me a lecture, he says, "Should we get you some dinner?" I start to laugh and nod.

"Grab what you need; we're going out."

I go to my room to grab a sweatshirt in case it's cold in the restaurant. I look at my phone and see texts from Dean. I don't open them. I can't. At least not right now. I toss my phone on my bed and follow Dad to the car.

Dad is like a quiet, calm, introverted version of Steve Jobs—meaning he seriously looks so much like him that it's a little crazy sometimes. He's even been asked before if they're related, and to be honest, sometimes I pretend they are. Although Dad is driven and loves to work, he does it quietly, behind the scenes, and doesn't have that same "it" thing that Steve Jobs had. He saves all his "silly" for me, which makes it even more special. Dad sings quietly to the radio all the way to the restaurant, and by the time the hostess seats us, the world doesn't seem quite so bleak. I order a cheeseburger, fries, and a shake, and we dip our fries into the shakes. We talk about how much that grosses Mom and Violet out, and a wave of missing them both washes over me so strongly that the tears almost start again.

On the way home, Dad finally says, "Okay, El Belle, it's either me or Mom. Who do you want to talk to? She'll be calling in a few minutes to say goodnight, and it doesn't matter to me who, but you need to talk it out." I groan loudly enough that it makes Dad smile.

"Come on now, no matter what happened, Mom and I still love you." I roll my eyes and then wish I'd waited to do this after his next comment. "At least that's how I feel until you tell me what happened. Who knows, maybe I'll change my mind."

"Dad!" I say and swat his arm. He laughs, and for some reason, it feels like maybe it will be okay after all.

Chapter Fourteen

UP AND DOWN THE KEYS

It is actually NOT okay!

I ignored the texts from Dean last night and instead talked to Mom on the phone until I fell asleep, waking a couple of hours later with the dark phone still next to me. I'm not sure how long Mom stayed on. When I woke up this morning, I could hear the birds outside chirping and decided that it was another new day and everything would have a fresh start.

I get out of bed, pull on the silky robe that matches my pajamas that Mom brought back from one of her trips to Japan, and sit down in front of my mirror to begin my morning ritual of brushing out my hair in front of my mirror, while I watch the window to see Zane drive by. But as I sit there brushing, instead of seeing Zane's car, I see Dean walking across the lawn with a piece of paper in his hand. I duck my head down so he can't see me, then wonder if he already has.

I'm not sure why I'm ducking from Dean, but I don't usually see Dean in the morning, and for as long as we've been friends, he doesn't usually come over. I wait for the doorbell to ring, but it doesn't. Then, when I'm sure he's made it back to his house, I peek my head back up and look out the window just in time to see the back of Zane's car passing our house. I let out a sigh and go into the bathroom. Okay, so maybe everything isn't back to normal, but I still have a chance at a good day, right? I stand at the bathroom counter, running piano scales through my head, the minty taste fills my mouth as I brush my teeth, then go to the front door to see what the paper was that Dean had been holding.

I open the door carefully. Every kid in the neighborhood should be at school unless they will be tardy, but still, I really don't need everyone to know, even if it is just the nice old lady across the street, that I wear a kitty cat pajama robe combo. Even at 13, I'm short enough to still wear clothes from the kid's section. Although my kitty cat phase has long been over, when my mom found these, she was sure I'd want them. And to be honest, I love them. They are incredibly soft, and whenever Mom's gone, I wear them and feel closer to her. I look both ways and after being sure the coast is clear, I grab the folded paper, clearly torn from a school notebook, on the doormat and close the door.

Elody,
Please answer my texts.
I want to talk to you.
Dean

    You'd think that for all the talking Dean does, he'd have a little more to say on paper. But he doesn't. I go get my phone and find that it's dead, so instead of reading texts, I plug it in, get dressed, and start my piano practice. Since Dad works with companies across the country, he always has weird work hours. So, I pretty much am in charge of my schedule. I love practicing the piano first thing in the morning. It makes me feel like no matter what happens during the day, I've done something well. I practice my scales running up and down the keys; it's mindless, and before long, my mind wanders back to Dean's note. Curiosity nudges at the back of my mind until finally, I stand up from the piano and go back to my phone, still plugged into the wall at the kitchen counter.
    I lean on the counter and unlock the phone. 27 unread messages. There are two from Mom, one saying goodnight, she must have sent that after I fell asleep, and another saying good morning. Two from Violet, one asking if I'd talked to Mom yet and another recommending a new brand of shampoo that has apparently made her hair look like commercials,

Up and Down the Keys

and 23 from Dean. I sigh and read the first one, then the second, then skim the rest. I'm not sure why Dean feels so responsible for my embarrassing display, but apparently, he does because at least ten of them say, "I'm sorry." Still feeling as if there's a chance at saving this day and making it better than yesterday, I decide that as soon as I hear him outside, I'll go over and reassure him that I am just fine, had a moment of weakness, and will never attempt to play basketball again.

I just don't know how I'll ever face Zane again. I mean, maybe he didn't notice. Maybe he thought a bug had flown into my eye, or I was having some kind of seizure or something. Yes! That's it! I'll have Dean convince him that I have some kind of medical condition that . . . causes me to scream when basketballs are passed to me? Ugh. Why do I have to be so socially awkward sometimes? I go back to the piano and pound out every desperate love song I know. Nothing seems right. Each one makes me feel a little worse than the last until, finally, I give up.

By this time, I realize I've wasted most of my morning, so I turn on my computer and begin going through my lessons. Conveniently, it's just in time to watch Dad walk in with his phone attached to his ear. He gives me a silent kiss on the head and grabs a banana, then heads back to his office, completely unaware of the notebook with 542 poorly written love poems that sit next to me in my stack of books.

My phone pings.

VIOLET: ELODY, TALK TO MOM!!!
ME: I did last night.
VIOLET: And? Are you in?!?!
ME: I don't think we are talking about the same thing.
VIOLET: What did you talk about?

I pause. Do I really want to go into it again? No. I decide not to tell Violet.

ME: Just my day, why?
VIOLET: Ehhhh, call Mom! P.S. That shampoo is really amazing! Add it to the shopping list. You seriously have to try it.

I thumbs up her message and text Mom.

No answer.

I think it's the middle of the night wherever she is anyway.

The day seems to drag on, my lessons seeming slower than usual. I can't keep my mind focused—instead, my mind wanders down the street to a house I've never been in. I wonder for the millionth time if Zane could get over my strange performance yesterday. Finally, with relief, I hear the thud, thud, swish of Dean's basketball and go outside.

Dean was obviously watching the door because as soon as I walk out, he's walking across the lawn toward me.

"Elody, I'm so sorry!" he says and wraps his arms around me in a hug that's slightly awkward since we've never actually hugged before but also kind of comforting.

"Dean, it isn't your fault. I'm the stupid one who thought for a minute that I could play basketball."

"But I shouldn't have let Zane make you play. I know how you hate playing sports."

"Zane didn't make me. He wanted me to play. It's my fault for being so stupid and making a fool of myself." Dean pulls back and tilts his head. A look I can't place crosses his face.

"Wait, Elody, do you . . ."

I feel the blush before he can even finish the sentence. This secret that I have held so close for the last hundred weeks feels like it's about to burst out. I fumble, trying to catch it, but like Dad says, all my emotions are displaying themselves proudly on my face without me having to say a word.

"Oh," Dean is quiet, processing. Then he pulls away. "Zane. Huh. That explains . . ." Then he turns away and walks back to his driveway. In confusion, I follow, take my seat against the tree, and watch him.

"Dean, it doesn't change anything for us."

He glances over at me before sinking a three-pointer.

"Yeah, sure, of course not."

But it did change something, and the rest of the afternoon is awkward. I try a few times to get him to talk like he normally does, even trying to bring up what he was going to tell me a few days ago, but nothing works, and it's almost a relief when his mom sends her dinner text. I wave goodbye and go inside, happy to close the door behind me. So, not only have I embarrassed myself in front of the king of my crush castle, but now I've ruined the only real friendship I have.

Chapter Fifteen

SMASHING MY DREAMS

All evening, an icky feeling gnaws at me. I pound on the piano for a solid hour, everything from Elton John's "I'm Still Standing" to Beethoven's "Moonlight Sonata," trying to erase the unpleasant feeling deep inside of me. Finally, after I crawl into bed, I decide I can't sleep without saying something to Dean. I text him, asking if he's still up, and stare at the phone, waiting for him to respond, and apparently, it's his turn to ignore my texts. I don't text twenty-three of them like he did, just one. I wait and watch until finally, three dots appear, and I sit up at attention, waiting, urging him through the phone, through the walls of my house across the yard, through the walls of his house, to answer me. But then the dots disappear. When I'm sure he's not going to answer, I give up and call Mom to say goodnight. She asks about my day, and I tell her about my classes, but for some reason, I can't tell her about Dean, really, because I can't quite figure out what to say.

"Mom, Violet keeps asking me to talk to you. What's going on?"

I can almost hear Mom's smile on the other side of the world.

"Oh yes, I'm glad you reminded me. Sorry, I got distracted with the whole basketball thing yesterday."

I groan inwardly. Can we forget about it already?

"Well . . ."

"So Violet called. She found this school near her that does a summer music academy. She wants you to come live with them and attend it. I sent the information to Mrs. Cleary, and she said she would fully endorse the program and even write a letter of recommendation for you. She is confident this would be a good fit for you."

I can't help the smile that spreads over my face. Live with Violet and Ethan? For the whole summer? And attend a music academy?

"Did you tell her yes?" I ask excitedly.

"I told her Dad and I are okay with it but that it would be up to you."

"YES! I want to go. I'll call her and tell her yes."

"Okay, okay, the thing is, Elody, there is an application required for the program . . . and part of that is an audition."

Smashing My Dreams

Ugh. My stomach drops so fast I don't even need a roller coaster to feel sick. This stupid audition thing smashing my dreams and plans again!

Silence.

"Elody? Hello? Did I lose you?"

"No, I'm here," I say in a voice that might as well have come from someone being dragged across the floor.

"Honey, you have to get over this at some point," Mom says softly. "I really think you could do this, and it would totally be worth it."

Silence.

"Okay, how about you think about it, all right? We don't have to make a decision about it tonight." Mom says.

"Elody?"

"I'm still here."

"Goodnight, hon. Sleep well, okay? I love you."

"Love you too."

I hit end and flop onto my bed.

Chapter Sixteen

PUCKERED AGAINST MY PILLOW

That night, I have a dream. About Zane. I'll admit, this isn't the first dream I've had about the king of my crush castle. I mean, seriously, how could someone be your crush for a hundred weeks and NOT creep into your dreams at least once . . . or a few dozen times? Maybe I need to get out more and meet more people. I mean, I know Violet says that almost every time I talk to her, but we're really different, she and I. She was involved in everything in high school. And I mean everything. She was on the dance team and even subbed for the cheerleaders. I know that's really weird, but because she is so short (like me, at least I wasn't in that alone!), whenever the girl they normally toss in the air was sick, Violet would go sub for her. There is no way in all the universe that I'd let a group of girls toss me into the air! She did student government, co-started a service club, and, of course, she was in the culinary club, too. It seemed like everyone knows her, and she loves it that way. She was always inviting people over, hanging out with friends, cooking for people, and going to dances and sports events. I feel social if I walk outside to get the mail and wave to Mrs. Silva across the street.

Where was I? Oh yes, the dream. I need to get a wider range of options to imagine because, apparently, I'm rather limited. In my dream, the sun was shining bright, and it was perfect sweater weather. I was in my neighborhood, walking down the street past Zane's house, when I heard his voice. I looked over at his house, and he was standing out front. His head was tilted slightly, allowing his sandy blonde hair to fall a little over one eye; his dazzling smile was filling his face. There might have been one of those sparkly "ding" things on his teeth (you know, the ones from cartoons, like, doesn't Gaston have one in the old animated *Beauty and the Beast*?). I mean, it was a dream, after all. Then he called me over to him. We started talking, and it seemed super natural. I have no idea what we were talking about because before I knew it, he was even closer to me, and then he leaned in and kissed me. Yep. He kissed me.

I woke up with my lips puckered against my pillow. I'm lucky I didn't suffocate. I'd like to think dreams mean something, that this is some kind of sign that I'm going to date him, that he really will be my first kiss, but we can actually start with why would I be walking down the street in front of his house? Remember how I'm not exactly athletic, so I don't go jogging or walking . . . so there's the first problem. And then, seriously, do I even need to keep going? Half of me wants to close my eyes and revel in the dream; the other half of me wants to roll my eyes and get on with my day. Which is exactly what I do.

Classes seem light today, and at lunchtime, I'm almost done. Dad comes into the kitchen, not on the phone for once, and begins making a sandwich.

"Hey, El Belle. How's your day looking?" I love it when he calls me "El Belle." I used to hate it until I learned that *belle* means beautiful in French, and ever since, I pretend that he is saying belle with an e, and it makes me feel fancy. Of course, I have to pretend that I still hate it, so he teases me and continues to use it.

"Not bad. My classes were super chill today." I watch as he spreads the peanut butter and jelly with the same knife, little bits of jelly sticking to the knife being left in the peanut butter jar. That used to drive Violet crazy.

"Good. Any plans for tonight?" he asks, taking a bite from his sandwich, which basically means putting half the sandwich into his mouth. Forget feeling fancy. This is the question he asks me every

Friday. Ugh. Remember how I mentioned that Violet was super social? So, I think he just got used to having a daughter who had things going on, but I don't. Like almost never.

"Nope, just going to clean up a bit. Same as usual. Wish Mom was coming home this weekend."

"Yeah, me too. All right, well, I'll get on with my day," Dad says, popping the last of the crust into his mouth and wiping the crumbs on his face with a napkin. He turns to leave the kitchen, then turns back.

"Oh, I almost forgot. Mrs. Silva called. She wanted me to remind you about taking care of Frank Sinatra."

"What?"

"Ah, didn't I mention it to you?" I shake my head, so Dad continues. "A few weeks ago, she came over and asked if you'd be able to help her out. She is having surgery this afternoon and won't be able to walk for at least a week. She was wondering if you could walk her dog in the evenings until she can move about more. I told her you would," he says smiling, "since you don't seem to have anything going on." He shrugs and walks down the hall. Conversation over. I don't mind walking the dog–it's just that same issue of my lack of social life. Even if I like it that way, I don't want everyone else to be okay with it, too.

Then it hits me.

Walk the dog.

Walk the dog down the street.

Walk the dog down the street past Zane's house! Oh my gosh, my dream is coming true! Well, at least part of it is!

CHAPTER SEVENTEEN

THE SAME GENE POOL

After lunch, time seems to slow down. I am so nervous to walk past Zane's house that my dream keeps running through my mind like a worn-out movie trailer, and I almost forget about the audition and Violet's offer to let me come stay with them. Until Violet starts texting me.

VIOLET: DID YOU TALK TO MOM?
ME: Yes

    She can't help herself, and the phone rings.
    "Hey," I answer hesitantly because I know she will want to know if I'm applying for the summer program, and I just don't know what to do.
    "Oh, my gosh, Elody! Are you so excited?"
    "Uh, well . . ."
    "I know you'll have to audition, and I know the

whole talent show thing, but seriously, that was years ago, and you're so much better now! I mean, last week, I was talking to Dad on the phone, and I could hear you playing in the background, and I literally asked him what he was listening to! It was amazing."

"Yeah, thanks . . . but I just don't know if I can do the audition—"

"Elody," she cuts me off again. All of the energy in her is pouring through the phone. "Of course, you can, for real. It's no big deal, and it would be so fun to have you come all summer! Of course, I work weekends and nights; this business is so crazy, but we will fit in time for me to show you everything here. There are so many cool things. I know you don't love hiking, but there are some really great places to hike, and you can even take the ski lift up in the summer, so it isn't really hiking; you just go up, and you can see the view. And there are so many cute little shops I want to show you. And when I'm working, you can hang out with Ethan. I can't wait for you to get to know him better. And he is so excited for it, too. Please say yes!"

I'm exhausted just listening to her, and I remember for a moment how life was when she still lived at home. So much louder.

"I'm thinking about it," I tell her. I really do want to go, and I love the idea of getting to know Ethan

The Same Gene Pool

better. He is my brother-in-law, after all, even though I've actually only met him a few times.

"Okay, I've got to run. We just got through the lunch rush, and I have two errands I need to squeeze in before dinner prep. Can't wait for summer. Love you. Muah!"

I tell her I love her as I hang up, but she might already be gone. I sit holding the phone, wondering how we came from the same gene pool.

I feel so torn. I really do want to go, but even the idea of auditioning makes my hands sweat, and they start to shake all over again. I go to the piano and sit down. Surely, I can do this, right?

I pull out Coldplay's "Fix You" and begin pounding the intro. It feels so good to play, to put all of my emotion and frustration into the movement of my fingers on the keys. For a moment, I think I can do it. Maybe I can. Maybe I got this. Maybe I have progressed and gotten better enough that an audition would be just fine. I stop and set up my phone next to the sheet music and hit record. Then I start over, and before I'm even into the second measure, I'm off. My timing is wonky, and in the third measure, my knee has begun to shake. By the fourth measure, it sounds more like "Cold*pain*" instead of "Coldplay." So, I stop. I turn my phone off and toss it onto the couch. Nope. Not happening.

I'm Still Elody Elizabeth

It's Wednesday, so Dad drives me to my piano lessons with Mrs. Cleary, which go smoothly, but at the end, she asks if I've decided what I'm playing for the audition piece, and I tell her I'm not sure if I'm going to apply. Her eyebrows shoot up so high I'm worried they'll be lost in her hairline, but she closes her mouth, and when she walks me out to the car, she asks if she can talk to Dad for a few minutes alone. I know what they are talking about, but pretend I don't. On the way home, Dad is quiet for a while, so I'm quiet, too, waiting for what I know is coming. My stomach is in knots, not because of Dad. Because of the topic.

"So, Mrs. Cleary seems to be a big fan of this music academy, huh?" He asks so casually that I start to relax a little.

"Yeah."

"El, what do you want?"

"I want to go . . ." I immediately answer, because I do.

"No, I mean, what do you want with your music? What do you want for your future?" It's quiet in the car for a few minutes while thoughts spin in my head. What *do* I want? I think about all the things I could study in college, and honestly, I can't imagine studying anything else but music. As the trees fly past us, blurring my vision, I close my eyes and reach to the innermost part of my desire, and there it is. I want music. I want to create beautiful music, share music, and maybe even teach music. I love playing the piano so much. It's become a part of me; quitting piano would be like losing an arm. I wouldn't know how to live without it.

"I want to study music and maybe compose or teach after college," I say, feeling a calm spreading over me like a warm blanket.

"I don't know much about music, but according to Mrs. Cleary, if that's really what you want to do, this is the best way to get into a music program in college. Apparently, the recommendations from these summer academies can send your application right to the top of the pile, and El, I'm not sure if you know or not, but this program only accepts incoming freshman students. So basically, if you don't get in this year, you don't get another shot."

I didn't know. I thought, worst case, if I didn't get up the courage, I could just try again next year, but apparently, I was wrong.

"You okay?" Dad asks after glancing at me a few times. I nod and take a deep breath. Deep down, I always knew I'd have to make this choice. If I really want to improve, I have to take this step.

"Thanks, Dad," I say, and he just smiles.

Chapter Eighteen

FRANK SINATRA

It's part torture, part opportunistic, but I wait until school is out to go over to Mrs. Silva's. She is scheduled to leave at 4:00 for her surgery but wants to go over everything for Frank before she leaves. He is a Pomeranian named after Frank Sinatra. Mrs. Silva says when she first got him as a puppy, she listened to Frank Sinatra on the car ride home, and he barked the whole time. She is sure it was the puppy's way of telling her that he and Frank were soul mates. I think he probably just didn't want to leave his litter mates. But I guess we all get to believe our own crazy.

Ironically enough, as shy as I am, old people don't bother me. It's as if they suddenly become approachable and unable to harm me in any capacity. Which is probably true, although I have noticed that old people tend to say a lot of things that young people aren't allowed to say. You know, like make comments about people that would be considered impolite.

"Now, don't let him near that monster of a dog that belongs to the Browns. We both know that dog is not trained in any sense of the word. I don't want any bad influences on Frankie here. And don't let him near Evans's dog, either. That dog is part wolf, I'm sure of it, even if they do deny it."

I nod and smile because we all know that it's true that Dean's dog roams the neighborhood and is constantly getting into everyone's trash cans, leaving surprises on their lawns, and stealing anything left in the yard.

"I've warned them. One more time, and I'm calling animal control," she says, handing me Frank's leash. I know this is true, too, but Mrs. Silva has been making this threat since the Evans got their dog, but still, she hasn't once made the call. She rattles on, giving me instructions on how to cross the street and pull out bags to clean up after Frank. I nod and smile and try to keep moving toward and out the door.

"Good luck on your surgery," I tell her as a reminder that she needs to be off, but instead of closing the door, she starts talking about her upcoming medical procedure in detail, much more detail than I am interested in hearing, that's for sure. Frank whines at the door, pulling on the leash, ready for his bit of tethered freedom, and I move out onto the sidewalk.

"Well, looks like Frankie here is ready to head out," I call to her. "Don't worry about him—he'll get all the exercise he needs this week." Then I give Frank a little slack in the leash, and he is off, and I am following gratefully, away from Mrs. Silva's surgery notes.

Chapter Nineteen

ONE SONG, ONE ASSIGNMENT, ONE HOUR

The closer I get to Lane's house, the harder my heart pounds. I can't be caught staring at his house, so instead, I give Frank Sinatra more attention than maybe even Mrs. Silva does if that's possible. Finally, I'm right in front, but across the street. I figure that's safer. But there's no one around. In fact, their car isn't even in the driveway. A strange feeling of disappointment mixed with relief fills me. Did I really want to see him anyway? I mean, after that last embarrassing episode, why in the world would I want to see him again? I had decided I never did want to see him again, but after that stupid, stupid, stupid dream, I kind of do want to see him. Just because maybe it was a premonition, and maybe Mrs. Silva's asking me to walk Frank was really supposed to happen this whole time, and maybe . . . but as I walk away from his house, the maybes weaken. It was just a stupid dream, and even if I did see him, what would I say? Did I really think I was going to have my first kiss ever (minus the pillow, apparently) on the sidewalk at 4:00 in the afternoon? This is all so ridiculous.

At the end of the road, I turn around and speed up. I've decided Frank Sinatra has had enough exercise for one day. I get back and put Frank inside Mrs. Silva's house, hang his leash up, and turn to go. Just as I walk outside, I hear the familiar "thunk, thunk, swish." I walk over and sit at my spot by the tree, even though I don't have my notebook like I usually do, and I watch Dean. He is fully ignoring me, and that icky feeling fills my stomach again. How can he ignore me like this?

"Hey, Dean," I say when he doesn't look up or acknowledge me.

Nothing. Okay, this might be a little more complicated than I thought.

"Dean?" I say louder.

Still nothing.

I stand up and go over to him. He dribbles around me, but after he shoots, I reach up and grab the ball as it falls from the net. Somehow, like a full-blown miracle, I catch it and wrap my arms around it.

"Elody, what are you doing?" His stance is full of irritation—hands on his hips, head tilted at me, not looking me in the eye.

"Dean, I said 'hi' to you, and you totally ignored me."

"Look, just give me my ball, okay?"

"Dean, what is going on with you?"

"With me?" Suddenly, his irritation has turned to anger, and I wonder if maybe I should have left this all alone. "Every day you come out here and hang out, and I think it's because we're friends, but then as soon as Zane comes, you completely act like you're a different person. You don't even care about me. Have you really just been using me to get to Zane this whole time?"

OUCH.

I have no words because I really do like Zane, and I have for almost as long as I've been friends with Dean. And, I really do hope every time Dean is shooting hoops that Zane will come out and play also. But wait, that does not change how I feel about Dean. Dean has been my friend for a long time. I'm not going to let this ruin our friendship.

"Dean, hold on," I say, trying to figure out how to fix this.

"Elody, I have invited you to play basketball with me a million times for as long as we've been friends, and what? Maybe five times you've been willing to even try shooting hoops. And ONE of those times was my birthday."

That's true. It was last year, and I had stressed and stressed about what to give Dean for his birthday. Then, the day before, I came up with a brilliant plan. I gave him a coupon book with three things since he was turning 13. (I ignored the extra ten there because that was just too many things.) One song, one assignment, and one hour. One song, because even though he can hear me practice constantly from his house when my window is open, I told him I'd learn and play any song he chose. Strangely enough, playing for Dean is the one person outside of Mom, Dad, and Violet that doesn't make me nervous. He still hasn't used it but brings it up every couple of months, so I know he hasn't forgotten about it. One assignment, because he is always asking me to help him in his English class, but he never wants to actually sit down and study, so I told him I'd help him with one assignment. It ended up being his final research paper for English and was the first "A" he'd ever gotten on an English paper. And one hour of whatever he wanted to do, I'd do with him. He'd chosen basketball. I should have known, but for some reason, I agreed anyway. It was humorous (for him) and embarrassing (for me), but I honored my gift, and after 15 minutes, he told me it was okay if I just talked with him while he played. THAT was the longest I'd ever played. For a birthday present. And now, he's throwing yesterday in my face.

"Dean, I . . ." I don't know what to say. I mean, I'm not that great at talking anyway, but in conflict, sometimes I just freeze. It's like all the words that I'm thinking and all the things I should or need to say start swirling inside my head, mixing up until even I'm confused.

"Whatever," he says when I don't reply to him. "Can I have my ball?" I toss it to him because I don't know what else to do. He shakes his head, turns, and begins dribbling again. I can see he's still mad, though, or maybe disappointed, which makes me feel even worse. There are few feelings as icky as a person you care about being disappointed in you.

I have so many feelings inside of me, I want to run inside and hide under the covers of my bed, escaping from all of them. I turn to go and begin walking back to my house. But I don't because I can't. I can't let my crush ruin my friendship with Dean. I want to leave this all behind; I want things to go back to how they were. The comfortable relationship Dean and I had. I want to blink twice and rewind to two days ago when he was excited to tell me something.

That's it! What was he going to tell me? I take a deep breath, turn around, and march back to the basketball net. I realize how determined I must look, so I lean against the pole and fold my arms as if I'd just casually walked up.

"So, what were you going to tell me the other day? Remember when I was working on that poetry project for school?" (Ahem, or something else, but we really don't need to bring that up again.) Dean is posed for a shot but stops, folds his arms over the ball, and looks at me.

"You really want to know?" He raises one eyebrow like he's my dad about to chastise me for something.

"Yes?" I say hesitantly. I think I do. Oh, dear. Do I?

"I was going to ask you to go to the school dance with me."

"Wait, what?" My heart drops. I'd never been to a school dance. I'm pretty sure Violet went to every single one of them, and I just assumed because I didn't actually go to school that I wouldn't ever go, but even though there was a part of me that was absolutely terrified of the idea, there was a tiny part of me that also really, really wanted to go. "You were?"

Dean turns away from me and makes the shot he had been posed for. It hits the rim and bounces off. He follows the ball and calls back over his shoulder.

"But don't worry about it. Since you're into Zane, I figured you wouldn't want to go anyway, so I asked someone else." And there it is; my heart sinks to the ground like it's made of iron, or lead, or I don't know. What's the heaviest metal there is? Whatever it is, that's what my heart's made of. Ugh. Dean was going to ask me, and he asked someone else?

"Who?" I ask. I suddenly need to know. I'm not sure what's worse—the fact that I was going to go to a school dance with my best friend in the whole world, and I ruined that chance by having a crush, or that Dean would now be going with someone else. Why did that even bother me?

"You don't know her—she's from school," he answers dismissively.

"Oh, okay. That'll be fun for you," I say, trying to sound casual but failing miserably.

"You'd probably only go if Zane asked you anyway, huh?" Dean says and glances at me to see my reaction. If he was trying to hurt me, he did. He knows that's not true. But for some reason, him trying to hurt me makes me want to hurt him back.

"Well, if he asked . . ." I leave it hanging, not really answering at all.

Chapter Twenty

MODERN-DAY BEETHOVEN

Even though it's a new day, my mind is another whirl of emotions. It would be my dream to go to a school dance with Zane, and yet the image I can't get out of my head is Dean and me all dressed up in matching outfits, posing with silly faces while my dad takes pictures on our front lawn. I don't even know if I could make silly faces with Zane around; I mean, I'd be so nervous the whole time. Even thinking about it makes my throat get tight and my hands sweat. I'm sure I'd do or say something embarrassing, or would I even be able to say anything at all? My emotions swing back and forth from excitement and the idea of being on a date with Zane to full-blown panic that nearly sends me to my room to hide under my bed.

I'm distracted all through dinner, which is frozen burritos, so it doesn't take much concentration anyway. Dad is in and out of the kitchen as we eat. He's closing a big deal in the next couple of days, so he has a million people calling him (okay, maybe not a million, but an awfully lot because it feels like every time he hangs up the phone, it starts ringing again). He starts multiple conversations with me but keeps getting interrupted. It's probably better anyway; I have too much on my mind. My phone pings on the countertop, and when Dad steps out, I go over to check it.

> VIOLET: I emailed you the link for the audition requirements. Any ideas on what song you'll want to do? So excited. XOXO

I swipe over to my email and click the link. Sitting back down at the table, I scroll through the website.

It's amazing.

Like really amazing! It's led by university faculty with visiting musicians to inspire and coach the students. There is music history, theory, composition (maybe I could put some of those poems to good use), and performances by incredible musicians. Ahhh . . . it sounds so perfect. To think I could spend a whole summer fully immersed in piano. It would be a dream come true. I click on the application link and read the requirements. All the images of me composing music under the tutelage of a modern-day Beethoven get chased out by the words: RECORDED AUDITION PIECE.

I toss the phone on the table and get up.
I think it's time to visit Frankie.

Chapter Twenty-One

THAT. WAS. NOT. THE. REAL. ME.

I walk Frank Sinatra every evening for the next few days and nothing. No Zane (I can't believe that I really thought I might actually get my first kiss from Zane on the sidewalk because of a stupid, stupid dream) and no Dean. I can't believe he's avoiding me! Giving up basketball in order to not see me is a huge sacrifice. The images of my dream begin to fade, and so does my frustration with Dean. I miss him. I miss hanging out by the tree, I miss knowing what's going on in his life, I miss having a friend to talk to. I want to vent about this audition, and my curiosity about this mystery dance date won't leave me alone. Every time I hear the basketball thunk, by the time I get outside, he's already gone.

I try texting Dean a few times. It's Sunday, so I know he can't be busy with school, but no answer. I give up and take Frankie out for his walk with me.

Mrs. Silva has been recovering well, which means she's had enough energy to talk my ear off about the proper cleaning of the wound area (I totally threw up a little in my mouth while she described it) every time I pick up Frank. This time, I sneak in really quietly so she can't hear me, skipping over the areas of her floor that squeak to get Frank's leash. He must have a sixth sense, or maybe just dog senses; I guess that's a thing. Because as soon as I take the leash off the hook, he's there by me, ready for our walk. I hold the door handle tightly so there's no click as it closes, and I breathe a sigh of relief. Success! I've avoided all wound descriptions for the day.

"Elody!"

I jump and let out a little scream of surprise that comes out as more of a squawk. Mrs. Silva is standing at the end of the porch, tennis shoes and sweatband on.

"Oh, hi," I say, recovering.

"I'm not sure why I scared you—you were in my house, for heaven's sake," she says.

I try to smile, but I'm a little embarrassed. She's caught me red-handed trying to get out of talking to her.

"I thought I'd join you and Frankie today. My doctor said I've healed enough to start moving about. We'll have to take it slow, though." Inwardly, I groan. I'm not sure I can handle a whole walk listening to Mrs. Silva's surgery notes, and slowly at that. Ugh.

"Great," I say instead of all the things I really want to say.

She really is a nice lady, and I really do usually enjoy talking to her, but I've always had a little bit of a weak stomach when it comes to blood and stuff . . . you know, all that other stuff that I'm not going to mention because I really might pass out.

We begin walking, and I wonder if we'll be home by the time the sun sets—tomorrow.

But, I try to be nice and "uh-huh" through the conversation, meanwhile playing scales in my head, trying my hardest to look like I'm listening while not listening at the same time.

Mrs. Silva drones on, interrupting herself with comments to and about Frank.

"So before I went into the doctor, there was this growth that looked like a wilty eg . . ." Oh, no. I can't do this. I start singing in my head . . . "and when the bandages came off, there was this . . ." Oh, no. I really can't. I have to interrupt.

"I saw the Evans's wolf-dog on our walk yesterday." It might be kind of low since I know he isn't really a wolf, but it's one of the topics I know she will grab onto and hang on like a baby koala. And it works. I feel perhaps a little too proud of myself and my quick thinking until I realize we are right in front of Zane's house, and there he is.

I have been walking past his house every day for days, and—NOW he's outside? NOW, when I'm with Mrs. Silva and moving at a snail's pace, and her going off on the intricacies of wound care again. He's outside, NOW?

I can't decide whether to look up or not, but I can't resist. It's as if there is this magnetic pull that I've been cultivating over the last hundred weeks, and now I can't resist it. Besides, I want him to know I'm normal, right? I need to set the record straight that whatever "episode" I had while we were playing basketball, That. Was. Not. The. Real. Me. It was just an . . . episode. I take a deep breath and look up, ready to meet his eyes with a dazzling smile. But he's not even looking at me. In fact, I hear a vacuum. I think he's cleaning out his brother's car. I don't know if he's even seen us at all, which seems impossible considering everything—the incredibly slow speed at which we're moving and the loud, one-sided conversation that we're having. We move past his house, and I breathe a sigh of relief. Catastrophe averted.

We get to the end of the road and turn around. This is seriously the longest and slowest walk I have ever been on. I'm pretty sure Dad is going to get worried and call the cops because, I mean, he may need to file a missing persons report. It's taking forever! We finally start moving past Zane's house again, and I'm a bit relieved to see that the car door is shut and he is nowhere to be seen. He must have finished and is back inside. Much better.

Chapter Twenty-Two
THE SOLUTION TO WORLD HUNGER

Just as my heart begins to fill with relief, Mrs. Silva stops talking. This shouldn't be such a strange thing, but because she has talked non-stop since we left her driveway, the world feels deathly quiet. I turn to look at her. I notice how the setting sun behind her makes her frizzy hair glow like some female version of Einstein.

"Elody," she says in a very firm voice.

"Yes?"

"Are you going to leave that there? Please don't tell me you've done that all week. I am NOT the Evans. I clean up after my sweet Franklin. I will NOT be seen as someone who shirks her responsibilities in this neighborhood."

I hadn't even realized we'd come to a stop, well, because we had been walking SO SLOW. But sure enough, there is Frank finishing up his business, but not just finishing up his business, finishing up his business on Zane's front yard! I quickly look around, relieved that Frank didn't have the urge while Zane was outside, and fumble with the bag carrier on the leash. The bags are . . . gone! Now I totally remember using the last one yesterday, and when I got back to Mrs. Silva's house, I was so consumed with sneaking Frank Sinatra in I forgot to ask her where a new roll was!

"Elody, is there a problem?" Mrs. Silva seems completely annoyed with me, which is interesting, considering I'm the one volunteering here.

"Uh, the bags are gone," I say, holding up the empty container.

"Oh, for goodness sake." Mrs. Silva reaches over and snatches the bag carrier from me and inspects it because, apparently, she doesn't believe that my 13-year-old eyes can see clearly enough to tell if there are bags in the bag carrier or not. I roll my eyes.

"They really are gone," I tell her.

She looks at me in horror.

"I forgot to buy more," she almost whispers. Then, her eyes get even wider, if that's possible, as something dawns on her.

"What are we supposed to do?" she asks me, looking up and down the street to see if anyone else has just seen her precious Frank Sinatra defecate on a neighbor's lawn. I think she might break into tears. This old woman who has been frustrating me for the last twenty minutes now seems so fragile. Her neighborhood reputation is on the line, and I have to rescue her.

"Here," I say, handing the leash back to her. "You and Frank keep walking home. I'll run back to your house and get an old grocery bag. It will be all right. I'll be back before you know it." The relief on her face makes me feel as if I just came up with the solution to world hunger.

"Yes, that's exactly what we should do," she says as if *she* had just come up with the world hunger solution. She takes Frank Sinatra's leash (who looks up at us with an innocent expression despite the fact that it's his poop that has caused the problem), and the two of them begin shuffling down the street again.

Chapter Twenty-Three

OVER BEFORE IT BEGAN

Now, when I told Mrs. Silva that I'd "run" back to her house, I really just meant that I'd move faster than she had been because, as we've established long ago, I am NOT a runner. However, even at a normal walking speed, I return to her house, get the grocery bag from beneath her sink, and am back out the door before she is even close to the end of her driveway. I pass Mrs. Silva at the corner, and she thanks me profusely, cheering me on as I "run" by.

Panting, I get to Zane's yard and am relieved that it's still empty. Except for a lovely pile of rather runny dog poop five feet off the sidewalk. Why does Mrs. Silva need such a long leash for Frank Sinatra? I put my hand in the bag, bend down to scoop up the poop in one quick swipe, and to my dismay, instead, realize that this pile is perhaps the nastiest thing I have ever seen!

The poop doesn't come up in one clump as it

has before, and absolutely should. Instead, my bag-wrapped hand pulls up a very warm glob. As I pull it from the grass, I feel it squish from my fingers, dropping back to the ground. This is a disaster. Before I know it, I'm on my hands and knees, trying to use the edge of the bag to grab and wipe the poop while attempting to deposit it into the deepest part of the bag, which I then realize has a hole. A HOLE! How did I grab the bag with a HOLE, and *why* did Mrs. Silva keep a bag with a hole? The poop is getting all over, and the smearing has intensified the smell. My eyes begin to water as I dry heave, and just then . . .

"Melody?" I mean, it's not my name. I could just ignore the voice and pretend that I didn't hear because if someone had said, "Carl?" I wouldn't look, right?

Ugh.

I look up to see Zane, the king of my crumbling crush castle, standing just a few feet away from me. His face is scrunched in a perplexed look. One more heave rises in me, this time maybe because of the situation more than the smell.

"Uh, Elody," I say.

"Huh?" The perplexed look is now full-blown confusion.

"My name is Elody."

"Right, so what are you doing?" I realize now just how strange this looks. I mean, if I had a dog with me, namely Frank Sinatra, this might not be quite so bazaar. But as it stands from his point of view, it appears that I am kneeling in his yard, smearing dog poop around with a grocery sack.

"I . . ." Where do I even begin? How can this be happening? He must think I am legitimately a full-blown, crazy person. "Frank . . . pooped . . . it was empty . . ." Oh dear, "Not the poop, the bag thing . . ." I begin again. Then I give up. I just *give up*. I wad up the bag in my hands and stand up, feeling the warmth of the dog poop seeping onto my hand, then turn and walk away.

My life is over. My dating life potential, that is. Over before it even really ever had a chance to begin.

Chapter Twenty-Four

PUTRID SMELL OF DOG POOP

By the time I'm almost home, my eyes are stinging either from the putrid smell of dog poop permeating my hands or the hot tears running down my face. I can hardly see as I cross Dean's driveway to cut across to my yard.

"Elody! What happened? What's wrong?" Dean appears out of nowhere, or maybe he was there all along, and I just couldn't see him between the tears, which I can't wipe because of my poopy hands.

I stop and hold up the poop-bag mess but can't get a word out. Confused but not willing to give up on me, he catches a whiff of the mess and takes my elbow. He leads me to the dumpster on the side of his house and opens it for me. Then, without a word, he continues to guide me to his house, through the garage, down the hall, and into the bathroom. While I rub my hands under the steaming hot water, he pumps half the bottle of soap onto them. The tears begin to subside. I glance up at our reflection in the mirror to see Dean's intense look. He is so focused on my hands and the soap pumping it almost makes me smile.

When they finally feel clean, I turn off the water and reach for the towel.

"Hey," he says quietly.

"Hey," I reply.

I follow him back outside, where we sit on the front steps. He's quiet. Dean is hardly ever quiet, so it must be hard for him to hold in all his questions. But I find that sitting next to Dean, surrounded by quiet, might be one of the loveliest things I've ever done.

But finally, he can't resist.

"So, want to tell me what happened?"

I nod. And then I start in on everything. I tell him about Frank Sinatra, about Mrs. Silva, about the poop, about Zane (I leave out the dream), and then I keep going. I tell him about my crush, about seeing Zane every day (oh, I leave out the love poems, too), and I tell him how I miss Violet and Mom, and then I tell him about the summer music academy and about the audition. I talk more than I've ever talked at one time to any person, ever. And he listens, like really listens. Not how I listen when he's telling me about school, and I "Uh-huh" him. But listens like he really cares and as if every single thing I say matters.

Finally, after it's all out, I take a deep breath. I don't even know what to say anymore. I didn't realize I had so much I COULD say. I take a deep breath and look up at Dean. His arm has been thrown protectively over my shoulder while I cried, and now, turning toward him, I can see the caramel-colored specks in his eyes, and I realize how close we are. But instead of feeling weird, it just feels comfortable and feels right.

"I'm sorry I didn't tell you about Zane," I tell him.

"You don't owe me anything, Elody. It wasn't right how I acted. Zane is a cool guy, and you have every right to like him. I guess it just kind of surprised me, that's all," Dean says quietly.

I nod.

"Maybe I should have told you sooner."

"Yeah, then I could, you know, like, play matchmaker or something."

"Dean, you better swear on your life you won't tell him!" I blurt out, suddenly mortified at the thought of Dean mentioning to Zane how much I like him.

"Relax, Elody, I got your back." He smiles, and when I look back up at him, he's wiggling his eyebrows. I slug him in the side, and he doubles up in mock pain and real laughter. It feels good to be friends again.

"So, can we talk about that music academy?" he

asks when we stop laughing.

"Ugh," I wrap my arms around my legs and collapse my head onto my knees.

"Elody, do you even realize how amazing you are? I mean, sometimes when I'm shooting hoops, and I hear you playing, I have to stop just to listen because it's like I'm getting this personal concert, and I still haven't even cashed in on my one song," he says. I can feel the blush start to climb; even though it's just Dean, I am still embarrassed by the praise.

"But every time I try to record it, it's a disaster!" I confide.

"Maybe you're going about it the wrong way."

"What do you mean?"

"Well, whenever I'm shooting hoops, I'm not actually looking at the ball or even at the net where I want the ball to go into; instead, I'm looking at the backboard, at the place I want the ball to hit, then make the basket. Does that make sense?"

"Kind of. But what does that have to do with recording an audition song?"

"Maybe instead of focusing on playing the song, you can think about something else. Something that will be the end result of you getting in. Something totally unrelated to the song."

"You mean, like painting nails with Violet on Saturday mornings? Or hanging out with Ethan?"

"Yeah, exactly. I mean, I don't play the piano or anything, but it isn't like every time I dribble, I think about what my hands are doing; I just do it. Is that how it is with piano?"

"It is when I know the song well," I answer slowly. Maybe this could work . . .

"It's worth a try, right?" Dean asks, and his face is so earnest there's only one answer I can give him.

"Yeah, of course it is."

He smiles like I just told him he's the world's smartest man alive, and I have a sudden urge to hug him. Instead, I side-bump him.

"Thanks, Dean—for everything."

"Hey, that's what friends are for, right?"

I nod, even though I don't really know. Dean is the only real friend I've ever had.

"Now, can I PLEASE get some shots in before my mom calls me for dinner?" He jumps up and is already dribbling before I can answer. I stay on the step and watch him. He must feel good because he's sinking every shot, but within minutes, his phone chimes.

"That's it for me!" he says. I stand up to head home, and when he gets to me, I reach out and hug him because it feels like the right thing to do. It catches him off guard, but then he hugs me back, and in that moment, the whole world seems to be just about right.

Chapter Twenty-Five

LIKE COCKROACHES FROM THE LIGHT

All night, I feel strangely content. I still have moments when flashes of Zane's face and the smell of dog poop sneak back into my mind, but every time, I try to blur them out with the feeling of Dean's hug. In fact, I can't stop thinking about Dean, which is weird because it's, well, Dean. It makes me incredibly happy. I begin to doze off with visions of hugs from Dean until my cozy thoughts are bombarded with a giant "YIELD" sign. The school dance. Dean said he asked someone, and now I need to know who. I bolt up in the darkness, sleep fleeing from my mind like cockroaches from the light.

Ew, that's so disgusting. I'm not sure why that simile popped into my mind. Speaking of disgusting, I suddenly get a whiff of the poop. I smell my hands and my hair, then climb out of bed, find my shoes, and smell those too—nothing. Could the smell be in my nostrils? Like little particles of dog poop clinging to the sides of my nostrils, ready to be activated at a moment's notice. That's it! I can't take it. I head to the bathroom and take a shower, hot with lots of smelly body wash, the one that Violet got me for Christmas that smells a little too "perfumy" for my taste. Nothing is too strong now.

By the time I'm in pajamas (new ones) with my wet hair wrapped in a towel, I'm tired. Too tired to worry about any boy, crush—friend or not—and fall asleep.

I wake up to my phone ringing. It's still dark out, and I groggily pick it up.

"Hello," I say without opening my eyes.

"Elody! Hi, it's Mom." Her voice sounds as if she's been awake for hours. Oh wait, different time zone; she probably has been.

"Hey, Mom! What time is it?" I rub my eyes and pull the phone away from my face, trying to make my eyes focus on the screen. 4:45 a.m.

"Early. I'm sorry, honey. I tried to call Dad, but you know how he always sleeps right through his phone ringing. So, my flight got changed, impending storms, cancellations, long story. Anyway, they were able to rebook me on another flight, but I'll be home today instead of this weekend."

"Today?" I ask, feeling suddenly awake. "Like, when we wake up?"

I can hear Mom laugh.

"Well, I'll be there close to lunchtime. I'm about to get on the plane, though, so I just wanted to give you the info. I'm never sure if Dad checks his texts when work is busy."

"Yay! Mom, I'm so excited!" I turn on the lamp on my bedside table and scramble to find a pencil and something to write on. "Okay, go ahead," I say, pencil poised above the back of the envelope. I think it's a birthday card from Violet. Mom gives me all the details—airline, flight number, etc.

"Okay, we're boarding now. I've got to go. I love you!"

"I love you, too! See you soon!" The phone goes quiet, and I turn off the lamp and snuggle back down into the covers with a smile across my face. It doesn't matter how old I get. I still love it when my mom comes home.

CHAPTER TWENTY-SIX

A MINGLE OF DEPRESSING NOTES

Even though Mom tries to come home on weekends, this stretch has been particularly long, and even though we try to talk every night, I really feel like we have a lot to catch up on. I try to persuade Dad to let me skip out of my classes for the day, but he doesn't budge. He goes to pick up Mom at the airport, saying that he can keep working on the phone and I can't. I work quickly through my list of assignments and lectures for the day. Before lunchtime, I'm finished, and they still aren't back. I check my phone.

DAD: Apparently delayed on the layover. Hanging out at the airport. I'll send ETA when I have one.

I send a sad face emoji in response, then head to the piano to get some practice in. Even though I usually practice first thing in the morning, I was so

A Mingle of Depressing Notes

determined to get my assignments done this morning I'd skipped it. Now, as I sit down, the audition creeps into the back of my mind. I pull out a simple piece by Beethoven, one I've been playing for years and can do with my eyes closed. I think about what Dean had said—then picture popcorn and movie nights with Violet and Ethan and hit record. I begin playing, and it's working; the notes I'm playing are actually the same ones as those written on the page! I start to smile as I realize I'm doing it! Recording a piece of music . . . for my audition . . . and that's where it all goes wrong. I hit one wrong note, mess up my timing, and my hands begin to shake.

    I glance at the camera and see my face, and immediately, I begin to blush. Really? I'm even embarrassed in front of myself? This is ridiculous. I keep going but really give up. I just start pounding out any notes I feel like hitting, and it's wonky and weird and ridiculous. I stop the camera and immediately hit delete on the video. How am I ever going to get this recorded? I go through a set of scales, then another, letting my mind turn to nothing until a question pops up. Application Deadline. Oh, shoot! Surely, there must be one!

    I click the link on my phone and scroll through. Sure enough. Of course, there is. Saturday, March 19th. Midnight. I flip to my calendar app and count the weeks. A little less than THREE weeks! The deadline is less than three weeks away! Nineteen days for me to conquer my crippling fear and record a song. I lean my head down on the keys, hitting them with a mingle of depressing notes. I won't be ready. I can't do it. I might as well give up now.

Chapter Twenty-Seven

STRANGELY JUST AS COMFORTING

When Mom finally gets home, it's after dinner time. Apparently, there were a lot of people trying to get out before the storm, and flights got overbooked, and then she got delayed on her layover, which caused all sorts of problems. She walks in, looking as if she hasn't slept in weeks.

"Hey baby!" she says, dropping her bag and wrapping her arms around me. Mom usually isn't gone this long, and until that moment, feeling her warm, safe arms around me, I hadn't realized quite how much I'd missed her. Mom's short, no-nonsense hair brushes across my face, and I breathe in deeply, absorbing her smell into me just as she says, "Sorry, I'm filthy, haven't showered in two days."

"Eeewww, Mom!" I tease. "And you're hugging me?" But I don't let go. She laughs, and we move inside with her arm over my shoulder, Dad following with her suitcase.

"Oh, it's so good to be home."

"What do you want first? Sleep, food, or a shower?" I ask. I know the drill.

"Shower, sleep, food. In that order," she says. A tiny disappointment niggles in the back of my head. I have so much to talk to Mom about, and I've waited all day for her to get here.

"Okay, I'll grab you a towel," I tell her, not wanting to be resentful.

"First, though, I want some Elody-time."

"Before everything else?" I look at Mom, her tired eyes and frizzy hair, and almost want to cry.

"Yep. We're long overdue, and that trip was way too long." She smiles at me with an apology in her eyes.

"How about you come chat with me?"

Mom showers, and I sit on the bathroom counter, legs curled under me, talking to her on the other side of the curtain. On and on I go about everything, even the things I've already told her on the phone, but she listens anyway. I hand her a towel and go grab her a drink before meeting her in her room.

"Mom, you sure you don't want to go to bed and we can finish talking later?" I ask.

Instead, Mom runs her hands through her wet hair, tucking it behind her ears, then climbs in and pats the bed next to her.

Strangely Just as Comforting

"Just come talk while I fall asleep," she says. So once again, I do. I can see how tired she is, but it makes my heart so happy knowing that Mom wants me near her. Before I can even get another story out, though, she's asleep. I tiptoe out of the room and shut the door behind me. It's dusk now, and I think there's a good chance she'll sleep all night.

Dad is in the kitchen heating up something in the microwave for us to eat.

"Hey," I say.

He pulls me into a hug.

"Hey, El Belle, she asleep?" he asks.

"Yeah, I'm surprised she lasted as long as she did."

"It's good to have her home, huh?"

"Yeah, it is."

We sit in silence while we eat, so different from the non-stop talking I'd just had with Mom, but strangely just as comforting.

"Thanks, Dad," I tell him as I finish eating.

"For what?" he asks, his face scrunched in confusion.

"You know, dinner, everything."

He just smiles and winks at me.

CHAPTER TWENTY-EIGHT

ALL ABOUT THAT BASS

I wake up to the savory smell of omelets cooking and the sound of Mom singing Megan Trainor songs, and I can't help but laugh. I may be musically talented with the piano, but that is the extent of musical talent in our house, especially when it comes to Mom. Dad can carry a tune and took piano when he was little, so he can play "Chopsticks" and "Happy Birthday," but Mom is as clueless as a raccoon when it comes to music. (Wait, are raccoons musical? Hmmm, I wonder.) Anyway, as I already mentioned with Violet and the piano lessons, Mom also has no sense of musicality and sings out whatever she wants as loud as she can, and it's actually fun and surprisingly liberating. When she's around, I feel like I can sing out too, even though I never sing out as she does, but it makes me want to. As I get up and brush my teeth, I sing "All About That Bass" through spitting and swishing.

In my effort to hurry out to hang out with Mom, I completely forget to watch Zane from my window and don't even think about it until after breakfast when Mom wants me to go over to Mrs. Silva's with her to check on her post-surgery. That's another thing about Mom—she has more energy than me, Dad, and Frank Sinatra all put together, and that's saying something since even though Dad and I are pretty chill, Frank Sinatra is not. Before the sun is properly up, she's already cleaned the house, made breakfast, and baked muffins to bring to Mrs. Silva.

We step out the door just as Zane and his older brother pass our house. I casually side-eye his car to see him waving. *Waving!* I can't believe it! He's waving at . . . Oh, right. MOM IS WAVING AT HIM!

"Mom! What are you doing?"

"What? That's Zane and Grant from down the street." She glances at her watch. "Isn't he late for school?"

I'm about to blurt out that it's a late start day but catch myself. I really shouldn't know his schedule, and I really don't need Mom to know that I know his schedule. Instead, I shrug my shoulders like I have no idea and don't care at all, even though I do.

I can't tell who is more excited to see us, Mrs. Silva or Frank Sinatra. Frank jumps around our legs, yapping in excitement as soon as the door opens, and

Mrs. Silva does the same. Okay, not exactly. She's not jumping with her age and all, but her voice seems to match Frank's pretty spot-on. She asks Mom all about her last trip, and then, of course, I get to hear all about her surgery for the umpteenth time. I zone out and walk around her living room, looking at the tens of pictures she has of her family placed on her bookshelves, the piano, and the tables, and I notice for the first time there aren't any children in the pictures, just some other adults with her and her husband, who I remember passed away a few years ago. It makes me kind of sad, but it also explains why no one ever comes to visit. On the way out, I ask Mom about her.

"She was never able to have children, and by the time they realized they never would, she felt as if they were too settled to adopt. That's why I always appreciate you going over and looking after her. I worry there's no one to check up on her while I'm gone. She's such an incredible woman, and there isn't anyone left in her life to look after her." Although she didn't mean it, I feel chastised. Here I'd only walked Frankie for a chance to see Zane, and now I feel bad. I get annoyed with Mrs. Silva for all her chatter, and now I realize she doesn't really have anyone else to talk to. Mom didn't go over to make her feel good; she was friends with Mrs Silva. I'm quiet as we walk back home. Maybe, just maybe, my life is a little too centered on, well, me.

The rest of the day seems to fly by with Mom around. She won't let me off the hook with school, but it's hard to focus with her moving about singing, cleaning, and making so many noises. I hadn't realized in the last few weeks just how quiet Dad and I had gotten. She makes tacos for lunch, and the afternoon is filled with errands I run with her. It's so nice to have Mom home.

When I check my phone right before bed, I realize there's a text I'd missed from Dean.

DEAN: Your mom home? Tell her hi.
ME: YES!!!!

Chapter Twenty-Nine

BUTTERFLIES HAVING A DANCE-OFF

Two days later, life seems to feel back to normal. Well, the normal when Mom is home anyway. I'm in my room looking for some sheet music in a neglected stack of books when I hear the thunk and swish and suddenly miss Dean.

I walk outside and sit near my spot, feeling the familiar comfort of the roughness of the tree against my back.

"Hey, Elody," he says without missing a dribble.

"Hey, Dean."

"How's your mom?"

"So good! I love having her home!"

Dean tells me all about history class, and how this girl was raising her hand, and how the teacher was ignoring her because he thought she was going to make a sassy comment because she's pretty sassy with him, but it wasn't a sassy comment after all, and how she ended up puking all over. He was laughing, and I was a little bit too, but I was mostly just disgusted, and for a few minutes, it felt like everything was back to normal with Dean. Then he asks:

"So?"

"So what?" I'd forgotten my love poem notebook, so instead, I'm trying to French-braid the grass near the tree. Apparently, we were a little overdue for a mow.

"Are you going?"

"Going where?"

Dean stops dribbling, holds the ball under one arm, and looks at me, squinting like he'll be able to read my mind if his eyes are half shut.

"You messing with me?"

"What?"

He must have been successful in mind-reading because I have no idea what he's talking about. So, he shrugs and goes back to shooting baskets.

"Dean, what are you talking about?" But he just shrugs. Okay, weird.

Right after, he gets his dinner text and takes off jogging toward his house.

"See you!" he calls over his shoulder as I head back home.

After dinner, Mom and I are looking at paint swatches for the kitchen while Dad decides to mow the lawn. (I may have mentioned the French braid during dinner.) Comparing paint swatches at the table, we try shining a flashlight on them, then we use my phone light, then hold the paint swatches up to the window, trying to compare the colors in different lights, when Dad calls in the door.

"Hey, Elody. You, uh, you may want to come out here." I look at Mom, who shrugs and then follows me to the door. There, on the doorstep, is a giant, and I mean giant, bouquet of balloons. Like a LOT of balloons, every color you can think of, taking up almost the entire front porch. There's a box at the bottom with some kind of game in it. I pick up the box/balloon combo and suddenly blush at the thought of all the attention that *that* many balloons in my hands brings to me. Trying to quickly maneuver the combo inside, I make eye contact with Dad, who gives me a smile and encouraging nod before going back to mowing, and then I awkwardly close the door.

"What's all this?" Mom asks.

"I have no idea . . ." I pull the card off the box and open it.

MELODY,
WILL YOU MAKE A SHOT AND
COME TO HOOPCOMING WITH ME?
ZANE

I may be standing inside my own house with only my Mom, but I can feel my face steaming like the sidewalk on a hot summer day. The box holds a desk-size basketball hoop.

"Elody!" Mom exclaims, having read the card over my shoulder. "Oh, my gosh! Hoopcoming! I'm so excited for you!"

What? Excited? I'm mortified and petrified, and what other words end with "fied"?

Zane and I have hardly even said a few words to each other. I mean, of course, I've wanted him to ask me out for over a hundred weeks, but can I really go to a dance with him?

Mom looks at the card again.

"Why is there a crossed-out M?"

"Oh, it's just a joke," I tell her, even though I'm actually not quite sure it really is. I mean, the last time I really saw him, that time on his front lawn, I would really like to have erased from my mind. Hmmm, I wonder if I could be hypnotized to forget just that one moment. Anyway, the last time he spoke to me, he actually *did* call me Melody, and I corrected him. But there was a lot of confusion, and it was a rather strange situation, so did he actually remember? Was this, like, an inside joke? Do we have inside jokes now? Or, even more embarrassing, did he *show* someone, and they corrected him? Oh, even more embarrassing, what if he showed Dean? Dean! Did Dean put him up to this?

Of course, I've always wanted to go on a date with Zane, but in my mind, we'd have, you know, gotten to know each other a little more before we went on an actual date and to a dance, too! Maybe talked with each other? Maybe said something more than just awkward words to each other? Was this because of Mom's obnoxious waving? Does he know I like him? And now I'm back to Dean. Oh, Dean! That's what he was talking about! How did Dean know Zane was going to ask me? Or, *more* mortifying, if Dean put him up to this, I'm going to . . . to . . . something.

"Elody, are you okay?" I have no idea how long I've been standing here just inside the door holding a giant bouquet of balloons, staring at a card with a misspelled name, and having multiple breakdowns in my head, but it must have been long enough that Mom had begun to worry.

"Oh, yeah, I'm fine. Just . . . Just . . . " I have no idea what to say. Just freaking out? Just having a mental breakdown? Just realizing that the thing you think you've wanted for so long might be just a little more than you can handle?

"I'm so excited! Let's go video call Violet!" Mom says. The excitement in her voice and on her face is *not* a good representation of how I feel. I groan inwardly. I have too many questions.

We make the call, and despite my reluctance, the squealing and excitement on Violet's part, combined with Mom's excitement, starts to rub off on me. By the time we hang up with Violet, the butterflies having a dance-off in my stomach aren't just because of nerves.

CHAPTER THIRTY

NOW WE'RE BOTH BLUSHING

I go to my room to get ready for bed and look at the card once more. But before I can do anything else, I need to talk to Dean. I pull out my phone and text him.

ME: Have a minute?
DEAN: . . .
         . . .
         . . .

I watch the dots blinking . . . and blinking . . . what can he possibly be writing? I mean, for all the talking he does, this boy is not the most eloquent when it comes to texting.

DEAN: . . .
        'Sup?

Oh. I roll my eyes.

Now We're Both Blushing

ME: Meet me by the tree.
DEAN: Now?
ME: Can you?
DEAN: Sure

I grab a sweatshirt, pull it on over my pajamas, and go outside. Mom and Dad are watching a movie in their room, so they won't even notice.

"Hey, what's up?" Dean materializes out of the dark, glasses on with sweats and a sweatshirt like mine.

"I didn't know you wore glasses," I say instead of something like "hello."

"Oh." He's embarrassed, and I'm surprised by this. I hardly ever see Dean embarrassed. "I wear contacts, but they were bothering my eyes, so I took them out for bed."

"They look kind of cute." The words tumble out of my mouth before I can even think about them, and now we're both blushing. He gives me a look that says, "Are you messing with me?" And because I can't quite explain . . . anything, I focus on why we're out here and move on quickly.

"Hey, did you tell Zane to ask me to Hoopcoming?"

"No, I . . . " he trails off.

"Dean! Did you?!"

"No, Elody, I swear. He was asking me about you, and if you would say yes, and I told him I thought you would. That's all. I didn't bring it up to him, I swear. I wouldn't, since I . . . " He trails off looking like he'd just been caught.

"Since you what?" I ask

He runs his hands through his hair in frustration, making it stand up in all sorts of places it doesn't usually stand up in, and I can't help but watch.

"Since . . . I . . . said I wouldn't," he finishes.

"Oh, right. You did say that. Thank you."

"But he did ask you, right?"

"Yeah. How could you miss the obnoxious bouquet of balloons on my front porch?"

He chuckles.

"And you're going to say yes, right? Since you're crushing on him?" He's watching me carefully, and I am suddenly feeling very confused. Of course, I'll say yes, right? I mean, I've wanted this for so long, and Mom and Violet are so excited, and Dean is going with someone else, but it doesn't feel the way I thought it would feel.

"Sure. I mean, yeah, I'm going to say yes since I like him," I respond. I can't figure out the look on his face, but the word that comes to mind is *disappointment*. "But I'll see you there, right?" I ask.

"What?"

"You know, at Hoopcoming, since you already asked someone to go?"

"Oh, yeah, right. Yep, I'll see you there." With that, he turns back toward his house.

"Goodnight, Dean!" I call to him.

"Night," he says, but he doesn't turn back.

Chapter Thirty-One

ONE THREE-LETTER WORD

All the next day, I struggle with how to reply to Zane. Mom and Violet have these grandiose plans of how to reply . . . fill his brother's car with mini basketballs, sidewalk chalk his driveway with a giant, "I'd be *hooped* up to go with you," send a carrier pigeon. Just kidding, that one was mine. They were getting so extreme I thought I'd throw that one in, and they didn't even blink at the absurdity of it. Finally, while they are still on video call scheming, I take a single balloon from the bouquet, one that is still rising with helium, write "YES" on it with a marker, and walk it to his house. I tie it to a rock and set it on his front porch with all the stealth I can muster. My hands are shaking as I sneak away, and I wonder how I'm going to actually go to a dance with a boy I can't even say one three-letter word to.

CHAPTER THIRTY-TWO

VERY SOCIALLY INEPT

"Mom, it really isn't that big of a deal. I'll just wear something from my closet." I tell her over the lumpy snowman pancakes drenched in syrup that she's made for breakfast. She holds her mug of tea with both hands up to her mouth and raises her eyebrows at me over the edge of it.

"Yes, it is a big deal. And you don't have a choice in this matter. I'm playing my 'I'm the mom' card, and we're going shopping."

Zane had called last night. I'd tried so hard to act normal when I saw an unknown number come up on my phone. We'd been in the living room, the three of us comfortably lounging on the couch, while Mom was showing me some of the pictures from her last trip and telling Dad and me about her research. I'd jumped up, nearly dropping my phone when it rang and left the room so fast that Mom ended up following me to my room to see if I was okay.

"Hello?" I'd squeaked. His voice was smooth, just like expected, and my insides instantly began to melt.

"Hey, Eh Lody." He emphasized the "Eh," making my name sound like two different words. "It's Zane, so Hoopcoming, huh? You ready for this?" I imagined his smile and maybe a wink with his question. "You there?" And then, after realizing that in my imaginings, I'd forgotten to answer, I gave Mom, who was standing in my doorway, a thumbs up and slowly closed the door on her.

"Zane," I cleared my throat. "Yes, hello. Hi. Hoopcoming. Yes. Ready!" Oh, dear. It would be really great right now if I could put even just a few words together to create a sentence that sounded halfway intelligent. There is silence on the other line. Maybe he'd changed his mind. Maybe he had second thoughts about asking a very socially inept girl he doesn't even know to a dance at a school where he will be surrounded by all his really cool socially-balanced friends. I take a deep breath, close my eyes, and try again.

"Zane, thank you for asking me. I'm excited to go with you to Hoopcoming." There now, that wasn't so hard, was it? I mean, perhaps it sounded a little like I was reading the script in a really poorly acted movie, but at least they were complete sentences.

"Cool. Yeah, well, we'll pick you up at 7:30 if

that's okay. Unless you'd rather skip dinner?" Was this a real question, or was this a "how do I get out of this" kind of question?

"I'm up for whatever works best for you," I say.

"Yeah, all right then, 7:30. We'll get some dinner and then head to the dance."

"Great."

"Right, okay. Oh, and Eh Lody," he says it weirdly again with a pause in between the syllables. Is he trying to remember it? *Do* we have an inside joke? Or does he really not realize how to say my name? "It's a whole matching thing for this dance, so, like, my mom wants to know what color dress you will be wearing so we can order a tie that matches."

"Oh, right, a dress." I hadn't even thought about a dress and matching, and then my face is suddenly hot. Just thinking about being around all of the other people at the dance with a dress on that matches Zane makes me suddenly want to curl into a ball. This was all so much easier when it was just in my imagination, not really going to happen.

"Okay, uh, I'm not sure." I frantically think through the few dresses in my closet. Mostly blue, I guess—I love blue. Should I tell him I'll call him back? No, I don't know if I can handle another awkward conversation. "Blue," I blurt out. "My dress is blue."

"Right, okay. Blue. I'll let my mom know. Cool. See you in a few weeks then."

"Bye."

Why couldn't we just text? Texting is sooo much easier. I don't have to actually talk for one, perhaps the big one, I guess. But also, I can take a minute and think before having to actually, well, communicate.

I hadn't even told Mom for this very reason. I didn't want it to be a big deal. I didn't want to go shopping for a dress. I'd prefer to go through my closet and find an old recital dress that I could still wiggle into. They might be a little tight, or maybe I could find one of Violet's old dresses. It'd be fine. But apparently, last night, Violet and Mom had been talking on the phone, and Violet asked Mom if they'd already chosen my dress. So that's why, while I'm eating my snowman pancakes, Mom, who had just assumed it was a casual dance since I hadn't mentioned anything about a dress, jumps on me about it. When I tell her I was planning on wearing an old recital dress, she shakes her head seriously.

"Elody Elizabeth, how many times does a mother get to take her daughter dress shopping for her first school dance? And you think I'm going to let you wear some old recital dress? When was the last time you tried on one of those dresses? There is no way one would still fit you. I think not!" So now I'm going dress shopping completely against my will.

The entire drive to the dress shop, Mom tells me stories of all the dances she went to when she was in high school. At first, I want to pretend I don't care, but holding my grudge is becoming more and more difficult with Mom's stories. As a journalist, all of her stories are told with details that many people would have forgotten. Not Mom.

". . . And then we had a bubble-blowing contest right there in the backseat of the car! And my date blew so hard he spit the gum right out of his mouth, and it hit the girl in front of him on the head, sticking to her very teased and hair-sprayed hair." Mom pauses to laugh at the memory, and I laugh too. "Oh, she was so mad! We had to go straight to the bathroom when we arrived so I could help her get it out."

"Did it work?" I ask.

"Oh yes. I mean, it ruined her hair-do, but we ended up stealing ice cubes from the punch, and I got it out. Her hair-do wasn't quite the same after that, and she wouldn't talk to my date for the rest of the night, but we survived it."

It was weird to think of Mom as a teenager like me, going on dates and to dances and parties and rescuing some girl from the gum in her hair. It was weird to think of her having a life before me and Violet and Dad.

"Oh, Elody, I'm so happy you're going. You're going to have so much fun." But I wasn't as confident, and doubt niggled at the bottom of my throat.

"What if I don't?" I ask, almost as if I'm afraid that if by not having fun, I'll be disappointing her more than myself.

"Just you see—you will." She smiles confidently, the same way Violet does when she knows she is going to get something she wants, and I wish with all my heart that I could be just a little more like them.

CHAPTER THIRTY-THREE

A VERY SQUISHY FLOWER GARDEN

Just when we pull into the parking lot for the dress shop, Mom's phone rings; she answers it, and Violet's voice fills the car.

"Have you started yet?" My eyes grow wide, and I mouth to Mom, "You told her?!?" Mom smiles and rolls her eyes.

"We just pulled in. I'll switch you to video call when we get in the shop."

I groan.

"Elody, I heard that! Let us have some fun!" Violet calls from the speakerphone. The shop is overwhelming, like really overwhelming. One side is all wedding dresses, and the other side, filling an entire wall of the store, are racks and racks of colorful dresses. Pinks, satins, sparkles, all of it. Not to mention the mannequins filling the showroom area with dresses in a variety of styles. There's a pedestal in the middle of the showroom surrounded by mirrors for the bride or customer to stand on. There is no way I'm standing there with everyone in the store looking at me. In fact, if it wasn't for Mom, I'd turn around and walk right out. But Mom is holding my arm, guiding me as she walks between the mannequins, checking out the dresses. She stops in front of a salmon-colored dress with an A-line hem, and that's when I remember my conversation with Zane.

"Oh, Mom, actually, it has to be blue."

"Why blue?"

"So, maybe Zane asked what color dress I'm wearing so we could match, and I might have told him blue because, well, I have no idea." At this point, I might as well just give in. I'm so in over my head in all of this.

"Oh, I love it when the couples are matching." For as unconventional as Mom is, she sure does love this kind of stuff. Maybe that's where Violet gets it.

"Sorry," Violet chimes in. "I had to sneak out the back. I really should be doing lunch prep, but they'll survive this once without me." I'd almost forgotten she was on the phone.

"Violet, this really isn't necessary . . ."

"Oh, yes, it is!" She cuts me off. "Absolutely necessary. Your first school dance! Elody, I didn't even know you knew Zane. Isn't he Grant's little brother?

He was so cute when he was little. So you know him?" Mom hands me the phone so I can carry on the conversation, and she can search through dresses using both hands.

"I don't really. I mean, I see him around sometimes." How do I explain my crush? I mean, I don't want to explain my crush. It was hard enough to explain to Dean, and he wasn't going to jump up and down and squeal at every detail, and that was before Zane had asked me to Hoopcoming. I'm not sure how Violet would react, but I can imagine it, and I don't think I can handle that while we are in a dress shop surrounded by hundreds of dresses as if we'd shrunk and we're walking through a very squishy flower garden. Luckily, I'm saved by Mom.

"How about this one?" she asks, pulling out a dress with a sweetheart neckline. The bodice is covered in rhinestones and fades down to a swirly train. I can just picture the disaster that dress would create . . . me, walking down the steps holding onto Zane's arm, and as I turn back to wave to Mom and Dad, I step on the edge of the dress and bam! The entire dress is down to the ground, and I'm standing in the front yard in my underpants.

"No, Mom. I'd trip on it. Absolutely not."

"Turn me! I want to see!" Violet calls from her position on the video call. I turn her, being none too careful, slightly hoping she'll be as sick as I feel when this is all over.

"What about that one? No, the next one?" Violet calls to Mom as Mom sorts through the dresses.

"Way too short," I say as soon as Mom pulls it out. Now I can imagine the trip I'd take as I turn to wave, falling to the ground, dress around my waist, my legs sprawling out. Nope.

I hand the phone back to Mom since she and Violet are debating about another dress and walk to the back of the store. All of the really fancy ones seem to be nearer to the front, and as I sort through a few in the back, my hand falls on a dress that nearly makes my heart stop beating. It has tiny cap sleeves with a straight neckline, falls to the ground in soft folds, and instead of sequins and sparkles, it actually has a blue floral print. I love it. Like really love it. Like, I can't believe I found a dress that I can stand to wear, let alone one I love.

"Hey, Mom!" I call, but she can't hear me amidst the folds of another dress rack. I carry the dress to the dressing room and put it on, purposely facing away from the mirror. The zipper is hard to pull on my own, but when I turn around, I almost can't believe it's me. Little 'ol Elody Elizabeth, looking . . . grown-up. I stand staring for what is probably forever, with images of me and Zane waltzing across the dance floor flooding my mind. I don't know how to waltz, but this dress makes me think I could anyway. Now he's twirling me, and he's about to dip me . . .

"El?" I hear Mom's voice call into the dressing rooms.

"Mom, I'm in here."

"Did you find something? I have a few here for you to try . . ." she trails off as I open the door and walk out.

"Oh, Elody!" Violet squeals, and Mom reaches up to wipe tears from her eyes.

"It's perfect!" she says, stepping in to hug me.

"Elody, it's so you! Wait, hold the phone up so I can see better!" Violet calls, and we both laugh. I step back and turn so she can see the back, and once again, she squeals in delight. "It's so perfect!" We're still there for another half hour until I finally convince them I don't need new jewelry to match, but I compromise on high heels that I'm sure I'll regret. Violet hangs up and goes back to work, and Mom and I drive home with a strange feeling of contentment in the car. We're quiet, which doesn't happen around Mom much, but at a stoplight, she reaches over and squeezes my hand.

"I love you, El."

"I love you too, Mom." She smiles and looks back at the road as the light turns green. "And Mom?"

"Hm?" she murmurs while watching the road.

"Thank you." She smiles again because I don't have to say it for her to know that I don't just mean for the dress, her excitement, or for spending the day with me, but for all of it, and most of all . . . for loving me exactly as I am.

CHAPTER THIRTY-FOUR
NICE KITTY CATS

It's an early-release day from the high school for testing. Dean had mentioned it, but I'd forgotten since it didn't really affect me until the doorbell rang. I assume it's a delivery person, so I don't get up from the beanbag in the corner of my room where I am very much absorbed in Jane Austen's *Emma*. I've read it before, but that doesn't matter. I like re-reading books, particularly ones that I love, and I love *Emma*, especially when I get to the part where she finally realizes that she loves Mr. Knightly. Swoon.

"So this is where you hide, huh?" His voice startles me so much that I literally jump, *Emma* flying out of my hands. Dean stands in my doorway with his arms folded, leaning against the doorframe with a smirk on his face.

"What are you doing here?" I ask rather accusingly while glancing around my room. I'm suddenly thoroughly embarrassed by the kitty cat robe tossed on the kitty cat bedspread that I'd had for years. Dean has never been in my room; in fact, he hardly ever comes into my house at all. It is kind of strange when you think about it. I've been in his house plenty of times, but even still, mostly our friendship takes place in the front yard, even more specifically near the basketball hoop.

As I stand up, I slide the yearbook under the bed with my foot, hoping he hasn't noticed it. It is a little strange that I have yearbooks for a school I don't even go to.

"Oh, your mom let me in. When you didn't come down when she called, she told me to just go up. She said you were probably on a date with Mr. Knightly." He steps in and picks up *Emma* from where it has fallen on the floor. "I guess she's right."

I can feel the flush creep up my face, but I try to ignore it.

"How do *you* know Mr. Knightly?" I ask, folding my arms and raising an eyebrow in a look of suspicion.

"Hey," Dean sits down on my bed with a flop, and I'm not sure what to do. He seems so comfortable here in my space, this space that no one ever comes in but me, and it kind of weirds me out. "I have older sisters, too, you know. Plus, my mom is a huge fan. You know she taught 18th-century literature in college a few years ago, so we got to hear all about the weird interpretations her students had about all of her favorite books."

"I didn't know that," I say, suddenly taken back by this whole life that Dean seems to have that I know nothing about.

"So," he says, leaning back on his arms and crossing his legs, still so at ease. "I decided."

I stare at him, confused, still awkwardly standing in the middle of my room. I try to put my hands in my pockets since they seem to be just hanging at my sides, but I realize I don't have any pockets, so I fold my arms instead.

"You decided what?" I ask. Dean's smile clearly has mischief written all over it, and now I'm even more nervous.

"On my song." Oh, right. That poor decision I made to include one song in his birthday present. I try to act like this, too, doesn't put my stomach in knots.

"It's about time," I say. "I should have put an expiration date on it." But my grumbling doesn't seem to sway Dean. He just keeps smiling. "Are you going to tell me? Or is this a guessing game?"

He stands up, "I'll tell you. Come on, let's go to the piano." He waves me to follow him and begins to leave my room. "Nice kitty cats, by the way," he calls over his shoulder. I roll my eyes and follow him down the hall.

When we get to the piano, he sits down on the bench like he's going to play, but despite the things I don't know about Dean, I do know that he can't play the piano.

"Uh, what are you doing?" I ask. He pats the bench next to him, and I reluctantly sit down.

"Well?" I ask.

He lifts up his phone and looks at me like he's in trouble.

"You ready?"

"Been waiting all year," I tell him, but I can't help the small smile that tugs at my lips. Annoying or not, Dean can make even the smallest thing seem like an adventure. He presses play, and the intro to Coldplay's "A Sky Full of Stars" begins to play. I look at Dean, and his huge cheesy grin is plastered all over his face; then I close my eyes and listen. It only takes a few seconds for me to float away.

"I love that song," I say quietly when the notes have faded. I open my eyes and see Dean's face close to mine, very close and very serious.

"Me, too," he says a little breathless and turns away. He clears his throat and stands up, appearing awkward for some reason. With a small shake of his head, he puts his smile back on. "And that, Elody Elizabeth, is why I want you to play it for me for my birthday present," he says with his hands on his hips.

"All right," I nod. I've played versions of it before, but none that have been . . . just right. "Can I have a couple of days to practice?"

"Hmmm." Dean taps his lips with one finger, pretending to think. "I guess I can accommodate that. How about one week from tomorrow?"

"Deal," I say and reach out to shake his offered hand, a little giggle spurting up at his faux seriousness.

Dean turns to walk back toward the front door.

"You better get practicing," he calls back to me, then turns with a smile and a wink before stepping out the front door.

I go to my room and mark the calendar for next Thursday. *Dean's birthday song due!* I add some stars and hearts, then, because the hearts seem a little weird, I turn the hearts into flowers. My eyes keep drifting to the day two days after. *Application Due.* But every time I read it, my heart begins to pound, so I ignore it and go to my computer. After searching and downloading the perfect version of the song, I spend the rest of the afternoon at the piano, Emma and Mr. Knightly forgotten. It isn't too difficult, just some tricky parts I go over again and again until I feel fairly confident. I don't love the idea of playing for Dean, but that was also the deal. It was my present to begin with, so I have to honor it, and after all, it's only Dean.

Chapter Thirty-Five

LIKE THE DAM BROKE

All week, I spend most of my free time practicing Dean's song. I mean, it's not really his song, but the song he's picked. The funny thing is, I've always loved this song, and it's been on my list of ones to really learn, but there's always been something else ahead of it in line. But now that I'm playing it, I can't figure out why I didn't bump it up to the top of the list. I kind of become obsessed. I love the mix of the loud and softness in it; I love the chords that build and build and then almost take a back seat with the lower notes until *they* build and build and come full force. I play the full-band version on my phone, wishing for just a minute that I could be surrounded by all of the other musicians and instruments that really make the song something so much more than what I can do alone on the piano.

This totally makes me think of the audition

hanging over my head, but I try to push it out of my mind. Instead, I go back online and download some of the other instrumental pieces because I wonder . . .

Three hours later, Mom and Dad come walking into the house and flick the lights on, and I'm startled.

"Why are you in the dark?" Mom asks, coming in with her arms full of groceries. I blink, probably looking like a deer in headlights.

"I . . . I guess I didn't realize it got dark," I say, looking around in confusion. The only light on is the small lamp that's next to my piano—the rest of the house is pitch dark. Dad comes up behind Mom, his arms full of groceries, too, and laughs.

"El Belle, what are you up to?" he says, moving to the kitchen. He puts the bags down and comes back to take the bag from Mom, who is still standing near me.

"Honey, are you okay?" she asks. The look of confusion on my face must be worrying her.

"I guess time just got away from me. I was working on this song for Dean, and I might have gotten a little carried away . . ." I trail off, still amazed at how long I'd been consumed. "What time is it? Did you guys already go to the movie?" I ask, faintly remembering a text inviting me to go that I think I responded to. Did I?

"Yeah, and dinner too. I figured when you didn't reply that you weren't interested." Mom says, sitting down on the bench next to me. "Okay, show me what was so consuming that you ditched out on your really cool parents and a really lame movie."

I want to show her, but I also feel so nervous, even though it's just Mom. Mom and Dad had gotten an electric piano for me three years ago for this very reason, so I could record, use other instruments, etc., or so they said at the time. I think it was actually so I'd use the headphone feature and stop disturbing the peace and quiet of every moment of every day. But I've never really taken advantage of it, never used all the incredible features it has; instead, I just practiced like it was a regular piano.

"Really? I mean, I don't know—it's probably not that good. It's my own arrangement with other instruments, and . . . I was just messing around." I tell her. I can feel my knees start to shake, but even so, I actually do know. I know it's good. Like, really good. Remember how I said that I was really good at the piano? I am, and it's not bragging. It's a fact. And apparently, I think there is a slight possibility that I might even just be a tiny bit good at this, too. This. I don't even know what to call it. But somehow, all alone in the dark and quiet of my house, left with this project for Dean, I kind of created something. Like the dam broke, and all of my talents just came flooding out.

"Go ahead," Mom says softly. "I want to hear." I take a deep breath.

"It's really..."

"Elody," she says more sternly. "Just let me hear." I nod and take another deep breath. Mom puts a calming hand on my shaking leg, and I press the play button on my piano to play the recording. I close my eyes, trying to relax as I listen to the intro, trying to hear it the way they would, trying to just listen instead of critiquing every little note and every space between them. And—it's amazing. The music starts soft and simple, with just the piano chords softer even than the Coldplay version, then builds, instruments joining in; first, the violin gently in the background, then the cello, then the drums join in as it grows in intensity. Behind my closed eyelids, I picture a garden asleep, spring coming in fast forward, trees blossoming, fruit growing, plants bursting with fruits and colors, vines growing quickly and sporadically—but with purpose and determination. I realize that my legs aren't shaking, and I open my eyes. Mom is staring at the piano, her eyes open wide in surprise as she listens. Dad, at some point, has joined us and is leaning against the wall next to the piano, looking up at the ceiling, and I think I see tears in his eyes, and that makes my eyes water a bit, too.

When the song finally ends, Mom throws her

arms around me.

"Oh, Elody! Did you really do that? All of it?" I nod in her arms, still not trusting my voice. "It's amazing!" When she releases me, I look over at Dad. He's swallowing hard, and his voice comes out raspy and raw.

"El Belle." He pauses and swallows hard again. Then he tries to speak. "It's incredible. I didn't know that you . . . It's beautiful." I stand up, and Dad wraps his arms around me.

"I didn't know either," I finally say. "I just, well, tried it and then kept going."

"It's amazing," Mom says again, squeezing my shoulder. "Really, El, so moving."

"Thanks," I say because I don't really know what else to say. I am still kind of in shock that I actually created it.

The three of us are quiet for a few minutes, each lost in our own thoughts. Then Mom says, "Let's listen again." I push play, and the recording—my recording, begins again. This time, Mom stands up and starts dancing around the room, interpretive dance style. I can't suppress the giggle, and after waving me to join her, which I don't, she tugs me by the arm until I, too, am dancing around the room between bursts of laughter. Dad, meanwhile, is air-drumming the entire song, even when there aren't any drums playing (remember how I said my family is not musical?). Well, drums or no drums, Dad is air-drumming his heart out. There's so much happiness in me, happy that I created something I know is amazing, happy that I have these two crazy people as my parents, and just . . . happy.

Chapter Thirty-Six

MY LEG AS A PEEING POLE

"*Elody, I'm so sorry about this,*" Mom says, taking her bag from me and loading it into the trunk of the Uber sitting at the curb in front of our house.

"Mom, I already told you—it's okay," I tell her, even though if I look deep enough and long enough in my heart, it kind of isn't.

"I'm sure I'll go to more dances in my lifetime," I say.

"But this is your *first* dance, and I so wanted to be here to take pictures and everything . . ." She trails off and pulls me in for a hug.

"Dad will take pictures and send them to you as soon as he does, right, Dad?" I ask, looking over Mom's shoulder, which I'm still squished under. Dad winks at me and smiles as he shuts the trunk. Mom still won't let go of me. She might be crying now, and Mom doesn't cry often. "Mom, it will be fine." She

My Leg as a Peeing Pole

finally pulls back and looks at my face intently.

"El, you have the very, *very* best time, okay?"

"I will," I say, even though I haven't even spoken one word to Zane since the phone conversation, and I'm feeling very nervous about going at all, let alone being worried about having the "very, *very* best time."

Mom climbs into the Uber through the door that Dad has opened for her after giving him a quick hug and kiss.

"I love you!" she calls as the door closes, and the waiting driver quickly pulls away.

"I love you, too," I whisper. Dad puts his arm around me and pulls me next to him.

"You okay?" he asks quietly.

"Yeah, or at least I will be," I answer him with a tentative smile.

Mom wasn't even supposed to be leaving until next week, but one of her coworkers covering a story caught some kind of virus, and he called late last night asking her to come cover for him. My feelings were mixed. I already missed Mom and the way she made the whole world more colorful, but I was ready to not talk about Hoopcoming . . . even for a few minutes. She and Violet have been so excited about it—way more excited than I am. You'd think it was a wedding for all the talk.

Dad and I stand there at the curb in our pajamas

with his arm around me until the Uber turns at the end of the street, and we can't see it anymore. I'm about to turn to go back up the driveway when I hear Mrs. Silva's door shut. I look up to see her and Frank Sinatra stepping off the front porch for a morning walk.

"Is she off again?" Mrs. Silva calls to us as she walks across her yard to the sidewalk. I find it suspicious that even though she stepped out of the house after the Uber had left, she happens to know that we were out saying goodbye to Mom. Then again, why else would we be standing at the curb in our pajamas?

"Yep, duty calls when random viruses work their magic," Dad calls back as he walks across the street to visit, "one of her coworkers caught a virus and needed a sub." I follow, but Mrs. Silva takes a step back and pulls Frank Sinatra toward her as if whatever Mom's coworker has can spread to her as if we were the ones who were sick.

"Is there an outbreak?" she asks with alarm.

"Oh, no," Dad stumbles, "another journalist caught a little something. Just enough to make it difficult to finish the interviews, so she is taking his place on the story."

Mrs. Silva puts her hand to her heart and sighs in relief, then proceeds to tell Dad about her sister's friend's cousin who got food poisoning from a chalupa

My Leg as a Peeing Pole

she ate at Taco Stop and how we should never, ever, EVER, eat at Taco Stop. It's in between "chalupa" and "intestinal problems" that it dawns on me what time it is, and just a little too late, I hear a car driving closer and do everything in my power not to look from Mrs. Silva to the car. I know who it is. I know the exact sound their car makes as it passes my house. It is so embedded into my eardrums I swear I could practically recite it if the sound of cars was something you could recite.

Embarrassment floods through me like a rainstorm as I realize both my dad and I are out here in our pajamas and technically not even in front of our own house, but nothing prepares me for the next moment. How could it? Because just as I'm about to take a really quick peek just to see if Zane recognizes me in my kitty cat pajamas, my right leg suddenly feels warm. Too warm. I look down, and to my shock and horror, while Mrs. Silva is going on and on telling Dad about every person she knows who has gotten sick in the last year, Frank Sinatra has decided to use my leg as a peeing pole. MY LEG. As if he is marking his territory on MY LEG!

And now I can't help but look. My eyes flick up just as the car passes, praying beyond prayers that Zane is distracted, or maybe taking a quick power nap on the way to school and has his eyes closed, or maybe it's just his brother, and he took the bus earlier. But no, Zane, with his brother driving slower than usual (I'm sure to check out the spectacle), makes eye contact with me, and then I see his eyes drop to Frank, who still has one leg lifted, just to make sure any little dribbles left make it onto my soaked pajama leg. And, once again, I'm caught in an embarrassing predicament—thanks to that stupid dog, Frank Sinatra. My face is flaming when I look back up, but Zane has passed, and I purposely don't look back to see him. Dad, meanwhile, has caught on to Frank's shenanigans and is shooing him away from me. Only a little too late.

"Oh, Frankie, no, no! She's not a tree." Mrs. Silva tugs his leash and begins walking away, still talking to Dad.

"We better get inside," Dad says, taking my arm and leading me as if I were an invalid instead of a pajama-clad, peed-on girl who was just embarrassed again in front of the boy who has been not only her crush but also the first and probably only date of her life.

Chapter Thirty-Seven

ON A COOL AUTUMN BREEZE

All day long, I avoid Violet's calls. When she finally texts chastising me for ignoring her (okay, so maybe she knows my life has very little that can be so pressing that I can ignore her all day), I text her back.

ME: Lots of homework, trying to do some catch-up work.

VIOLET: I. DON'T. CARE. ANSWER MY FREAKING PHONE CALL!!!

Oops. I think she might be mad at me. I sigh and give her a huge eye roll, even though she can't see me, and call her.

"What in the world, Elody?!" she says without even saying hello.

"I've been busy!" I tell her.

"Um, I don't care— I'm your sister, and Mom

just left, and I need to be able to check in on you when I call."

"Violet, I'm 13 years old. Mom's been gone for less than eight hours, and Dad and I haven't left the house all day. Really, you don't need to babysit me."

"Regardless, when I call all day, could you at least just answer once?" she softens, maybe catching on to just how ridiculous she's being.

"Okay, fine. Here I am." I'm feeling grumpy at this point.

"Gosh, now I'm super excited to talk to you."

"Hey, you're the one who keeps calling!"

Violet's quiet for a couple of moments, and I let the silence sit, feeling all the irritation fly away like like leaves on a cool autumn breeze.

"Sorry," she says.

"Me too."

"I just worry about you sometimes."

"Why?" I ask, this time without malice, "I'm fine, Violet."

"I know, I just . . . it's just that Mom is gone a lot more than she used to be, and with Hoopcoming coming up, I really wanted her to be there for you."

"It's okay."

"I know. Maybe you're just not as needy as I was at your age."

"Yeah, that's probably it." I know she can hear the

smile in my voice, and she laughs, and we're back to where we are supposed to be.

"So, what's on your list for today?" she asks with a fresh voice, leaving our conflict behind.

"Violet, I really am doing schoolwork. I got a little behind while Mom was home, so I've been catching up."

"That's good. I'm glad you're so dedicated. I don't know if I could do what you do." I feel like she's stalling for a moment, and I can't figure out why.

"Violet?"

"Yeah?"

"What?"

"What are you talking about?"

"I know you have something to say; just say it."

"Mom made me promise not to say anything because you're getting too stressed out about it!"

I take a deep breath.

"It's the audition, isn't it?"

"I'm sorry, Elody, it's just that the audition deadline is in two days, and I know this would be so incredible for you, and I really want you to be able to come!"

The sad thing is, I really want it too. I just . . . I just . . . I just don't know if I can do it.

"I'm not putting any pressure on you," she says. Except that is exactly what she's doing. "I just wanted to, you know, check in and see if you are ready." I'm not. But I don't say that to her. I don't know what to say because every single time I think about the audition, I get so nervous that I think I'm going to pass out. I can just imagine myself on the screen playing the piano until my nerves get the best of me and then "thunk!" passing out right there on the keys. I'm sure that would impress the auditions committee.

"Oh, Violet, Dad needs me—I've got to go," I tell her and hang up before she can say anything else. Dad's not calling, but because I feel guilty for lying to my sister, whom I love and usually really like, except when she's pressuring me to do something I don't want to do, I leave my desk and wander into Dad's office. He's sitting at his desk on a call but waves me over to him anyway. After a few minutes, he makes eye contact and mouths "sorry" to me. I smile and give him a thumbs-up. I really don't need anything; I just needed to stop thinking about the audition for a while. I sit on his desk and begin linking paper clips together until I have a chain long enough to be a necklace. Finally, Dad finishes his conversation.

He stretches back in his chair with his arms over his head.

"Hey, El Belle. What's up?"

"Not much. I just needed to get Violet off the

phone, so I told her you needed me." He chuckles at my blatant honesty.

"She harassing you again?"

"Just about the audition," I tell him, swirling the paper clip train around on the desk.

"Want to talk about it?" This is one of my very favorite things about my dad. He never pressures me but gives me the option, which, for some reason, makes me want to talk. Like, because it's up to me, it seems easier to do.

"I just don't know what to do, Dad."

"What do you mean?"

"So, the audition and application are due in two days, and I still haven't even figured out what to play," I tell him, my voice a little high and sounding slightly whiny, even though I don't mean it to.

"Have you filled out the application yet?"

"No."

"Well, maybe start there. Maybe one of the questions will trigger something for you. You know, Elody, they just want to know the kind of musician you are and who you are as a person. It's not as if they want something you perform just for them, like one of your old recitals. They want to know if the person you are is a good fit for what they have to offer. They don't want you to come if they don't think they can help you grow. It wouldn't even make sense if they wanted someone who was already perfect at everything. And you're a pretty good pianist, so maybe show them your strengths and weaknesses. You can't possibly be the first person who has had stage fright."

Strangely, what Dad is saying makes a lot of sense. I think he could be right. Why would they want to accept someone who was already amazing at everything?

"Why don't you just start with the application? After that, see how you feel."

This was a lot coming from my dad, who doesn't say much, but it was also just what I needed to hear. I lean down and kiss him on his cheek.

"Thank you, Dad," I say, then turn to leave the room.

"El Belle." I pause in the doorway and turn back to him. "One more thing—just remember, no matter what happens with this music academy, you apply, you don't, whether you get in or not, in the end, you're still an amazing musician, and no matter what, you're my girl, and I love you." There is suddenly a lump in my throat. I smile at him.

"Thank you, Dad, I love you, too."

Even with the lump in my throat, my heart feels lighter.

CHAPTER THIRTY-EIGHT

I'M STILL ELODY ELIZABETH

I go to my room and pull up the application on my computer. I begin filling out the application form, all the easy stuff: name, birthday, how long I've been playing the piano, all that mindless stuff. Then, I get to the part that talks about the audition recording, and I feel my breathing begin to get shaky. I sit back, close my eyes, and try to bring back into my mind all the things my dad said. Deep breaths. When I really think about it, he's right; no matter what happens, I'm still me. I'm still Elody Elizabeth, with a mom and dad and sister who (although Violet will be greatly disappointed) will still love me, and that means a lot.

I think about Dean and the awkwardness recently after telling him about my Zane crush. Even his friendship wouldn't change based on this audition. So, what did I have to lose? Dean . . . my mind starts to wander, and that's when I realize that even though

I'd finished his song, I still hadn't played it for him. I was so concerned about getting it ready, and then the next morning, Mom left . . . and I totally spaced it. I look at my calendar and see that today's date is circled. I told Dean I'd play it for him by today. My eyes wander to the box outlined in highlighter pink. *Application deadline:* Saturday by midnight. Two days away. I go back to the computer and hit "save for later" on the application. Everything is ready except for uploading the audition recording. But I have two days to somehow figure that out, and Dean's song is due today.

I pull out my phone.

ME: Hey! What are you doing rn?

No answer. I check my clock. He should be getting home from school any minute. I could stay and watch Zane drive by. But I'm afraid if I don't act now, I'll lose my nerve, so I leave my room without even closing my laptop and head over to Dean's house. I'll wait for him there.

CHAPTER THIRTY-NINE

HUGS THAT FEEL LIKE HOME

When the door opens to my knock, it's Dean's mom, Mrs. Evans. She greets me with a smile as big as Dean's and welcomes me inside with a hug. I know I only live next door, but whenever I see her, she pulls me into a hug as if I'm her long-lost child, and she hasn't seen me for months. Where my mom is thin and wiry, always moving fast and talking fast and ready for the next thing, like Violet, Dean's mom is warm and soft, and it feels like home in her arms. Her house is that way, too; it has a homey feeling and always smells as if something delicious is cooking. Today, I think it's pot roast, and the smell makes my stomach grumble. I don't even remember if I ate lunch today . . .

"Dean's not home yet, but come in and wait," she says, leading me down the hall. "Tell me what's been happening, Miss Elody." She puts an arm through mine and walks me into the family room with the big overstuffed couches and rocking recliner. Everyone in Dean's family is big; even Dean's older sister is tall like him, and the furniture matches them perfectly—big, comfortable, and friendly.

"Not too much," I tell her, even though I'd had a tornado of emotions running through me all day.

"Dean tells me you're going to Hoopcoming with our neighbor. What's his name again?" she asks, oblivious to the butterflies that suddenly storm my stomach.

"Uh, yeah. Zane." I say as the blush rushes my face.

"Oh, yes, that's right. He seems like a nice boy."

"Yeah," I say because I don't know what else to say . . . that he's been my crush for a hundred weeks? That I've recently realized that I actually don't even know if he is a "nice boy," but I sure hope so because I'm now going on a date with him?

"I think you will have a great time," she says, and I realize right then that this might be the opportunity I've been waiting for.

"So, Hoopcoming . . . who is Dean going with? He hasn't told me yet," I say, trying to sound way more casual than I am. She tilts her head slightly as if she's trying to understand.

"You know, who's he taking to Hoopcoming?" I ask again, hoping to clarify. Maybe she thinks this is none of my business, or maybe she's surprised Dean hasn't told me.

"Oh, I thought you knew. He's—"

"Hey, hey!" A voice coming from the front hall interrupts her, and Dean walks in with his hands stretched out as if he has just won the NBA finals.

"What's going on?"

"Speak of the devil himself!" Mrs. Evans laughs as she stands up to let Dean kiss her cheek.

"How was school?" she asks him.

"Good, good! Elody, what's up? Are you here to deliver? All day I've been waiting, you know. Today is the deadline, and I'm ready to collect." He dances around like he's taunting me, and I shake my head but can't help but smile.

"I know," I say, "that's why I'm here."

"Sweet! Let's go hear it."

"Is this that birthday present you've been talking about?" Mrs. Evans asks, laughing. "You poor girl."

I shake my head. "It's my fault for giving it to him in the first place," I say, rolling my eyes. She laughs again.

"Rookie mistake. Never promise this kid anything. He has a mind like a vault and never forgets anything!" she says, moving to the kitchen, and we follow. "When he was three years old, I promised him I'd get him a dog when he turned eight. He talked about that dog every day for over a year until I was so sick of it that I went to the shelter and adopted the first puppy we saw. Still have that dang dog. Big mistake that was," she says with a smile.

Dean and I laugh. I had no idea of the background behind the dog that half the neighborhood hates.

Dean grabs an apple from the counter and tosses it up in the air, then hands it to me. The smell of pot roast makes my stomach growl again, so I take the apple, and Dean grabs another for himself.

"Momma, I'm off for my own private concert. I'll try to make it back before dinner," he says, grabbing his phone from where he tossed it when he walked in. She laughs and swats at him as we head to the door. I love the casual teasing that goes on with them. It feels so natural and comfortable, and I can see why Dean feels so relaxed all the time.

CHAPTER FORTY

SWIMMING IN A POOL FULL OF NOTES

Dean follows me across the yard, talking the whole way, and I do what I always do: mostly just listen. It feels so good to feel normal with Dean again. It's natural and easy, just like it used to be, and his chatting distracts me, so by the time we get inside to my piano, I've completely forgotten to be nervous.

Dean carries a chair in from the dining room and sits behind me and a little to the left. He rubs his hands together in anticipation and lets his huge grin split his face in two. I start to feel a little nervous as I turn the piano on, but one glance at the huge grin on his face makes me smile.

"So, this might not be exactly what you expected," I tell him. "I kind of took some liberties with the song and made it my own. And I kind of, sort of, recorded some extra instruments to go with it, too."

"You mean, you like, composed your own

version?" Dean asks in surprise.

"Yeah?" I say it as if it's a question, and Dean laughs.

"Take it away, girl! I'm ready! Happy birthday to me."

I roll my eyes at him and set my feet on the pedals. I push the play button and begin counting in my head as the music starts. I can't look at Dean, so instead, I focus on the music, listening for my cue to begin playing with the instruments I've recorded. I begin, and within seconds, I'm lost in my own music. I expected to be too nervous to play, even if it's just Dean, but I feel so deep inside the music like I'm swimming in a pool full of notes and melodies and instruments all around me, and it isn't until the end, until the last couple of notes, that I come up for air and that's when my heart begins to pound. The music dies out, and I still can't look up from the keys. Dean doesn't make a sound, so instead, I can hear the blood pumping in my ears.

Finally, I barely tilt my head so I can look up and see his face from the side of my eyes. He is sitting there with his mouth hanging open like a giant guppy fish. Then he lets out the biggest yelp I've ever heard and jumps out of his chair, startling me.

"Are you kidding me? Elody, are you kidding me? You can do THAT? All this time, I could hear you practicing, and it was great, but that? That was incredible!" He's on his feet, running his hands through his hair and shaking his head in disbelief when Dad peeks his head in.

"Everything okay?" he asks. I nod and smile. But before I can explain anything to Dad, Dean cuts in.

"Elody just played my birthday present for me—have you heard it? Were you aware of what she can do?" The excitement in his voice is infectious, and I feel all warm and giddy.

My dad chuckles, pride written all over his face.

"Pretty incredible, right?" Dad smiles at me, and I can't wipe the cheesy grin off my face. I just feel so happy. Happy because of my dad's pride, Dean's reaction, and honestly, because it is pretty awesome what I can do, and after so many years of diligent practice—it's kind of nice to feel like I've created something amazing.

Dad goes back to his office, still with a pleased smile on his face. He never pressures me to perform for others, but I know it makes him happy to see someone else get to enjoy and appreciate my talents. I'm still on the piano bench, and Dean sits back down. He reaches for my hands and moves close, so I have to look him in the eyes.

"Elody, for real, that was . . ." he pauses, and I'm shocked to see Dean at a loss for words. "That was really, really good. It was beautiful. You're incredible." Now, I feel heat rise in my face.

"Thanks," I say, back to my awkward self, and gently pull my hands away. I busy myself with turning off the piano and closing the lid, even though I never close the lid.

"No, thank you," Dean says. "That's the best personal birthday concert I've ever had."

"Oh, please. We both know it's the only personal birthday concert you've ever had."

"Okay, that may be true, but now I have a really, really high standard from here on out. Any personal birthday concerts I ever get will have to try to compete with this one." We're quiet for a few minutes, the excitement of Dean's reaction calming around us.

"So, can I ask you something?" he asks hesitantly.

"Yeah . . ." I wait.

"Have you recorded your audition yet?"

I turn to him and scrunch up my nose, making a face.

"No, and do we have to talk about it?"

"Well, would you consider sending this song?" he asks, nodding toward the piano.

"I'd love to," I tell him. "It's just that every time I hit record and start to introduce the song, my hands start shaking, and by the time I get through the first line, it's like a musical pot of gumbo."

He doesn't say anything; instead, he nods his head with a look in his eyes I can't quite place.

"What?"

"Nothing."

"Really, what?"

"Nothing. Why don't you show me the application? I want to see what they are asking for."

"Fine." I'm rolling my eyes again.

We go into my room, and I sit down at my desk while Dean looks over my shoulder from his place sitting on my kitty cat bedspread.

I pull up the website and log into the application portal, then click on the information button about the audition recording. The rules are pretty straightforward, and Dean and I read them together: "The song can be original, a composition, or traditional. It needs to be at least two minutes long. It must be both a video and audio recording." This is where I groan. The instructions encourage applicants to perform the best they can so the panel can see what they'd be working with if they accept you into the program.

"I don't see anywhere where it says you have to introduce your piece," Dean says after we finish reading it.

"No, I guess it doesn't. That's just what you normally do when you perform a piece," I tell him. "Regardless of whether or not I do recitals now, I have in the past, even if I do try to erase them from my memory."

"Huh."

"What?" I ask. Here we go again—Dean and his cryptic responses.

"Nothing."

I roll my eyes and then shrug.

"So, do you want to shoot hoops?" I ask, not really loving the fact that Dean is in my room looking around at all the decorations I've had since I was a little kid. He stands up.

"Actually, I have some homework I wanted to get done before dinner."

Oh? This was strange. Dean hadn't mentioned any homework that he was eager to get done, and he almost never did his homework before dinner.

"Okay . . ." I say, following him out of my room. He turns back to me when we get to the front door.

"Elody, that really was amazing. Thank you. It was the best birthday gift I've ever gotten." He reaches in and gives me a big hug. He obviously learned to hug from his Mom, and this, too, feels like home, and I choose to ignore his strange, sudden need to rush home.

"You're welcome," I say into his warm chest. Then he pulls away and runs out the door and across the yard as if the homework he has to do is more exciting than presents on Christmas morning.

Chapter Forty-One

MISTAKEN FOR RAISIN PRINTS

Dad and I heat up the last of the leftovers from the fridge for dinner. I can't quite remember what these were at one time, but the apple I'd eaten at Dean's house hadn't stopped the grumbling in my stomach. The house feels quiet. We sit down, and Dad asks about playing for Dean, and I can tell he liked Dean's reaction.

"He's right, you know," he says.

"I know, Dad," I say and smile at him.

"So how come you aren't going to Hoopcoming with Dean?" he asks. I think about all the drama that has been in my head since Zane asked me and seriously wonder now how it would have been different if I were going with Dean. Would I be as nervous? More excited? I'm not sure, but I think I have an idea.

"Because . . . I guess because Zane asked me, and Dean was already going with someone else."

"Oh? Who's he taking?"

"Actually, I don't know—he won't tell me."

"Huh, that's strange." And it is strange. I think back to when I asked Dean's mom and the look she had given me right before Dean walked in. It makes me wonder now if there is someone Dean likes, and maybe she was surprised that I didn't know about her already. The reality is Dean goes to school every day and has this whole life outside of us interacting. I mean, really, truly, Dean could have a girlfriend, and I could know nothing about it. And now that I'm sitting here chewing leftover unidentifiable something, I'm pretty sure of it. Dean has a girlfriend. And he is taking her to Hoopcoming. And Dean's mom was surprised that I didn't know because he's probably been dating her for months. I've never actually asked him if he has a girlfriend. In fact, we never have talked about girls. And although he tells me a lot of stuff, there's no way he tells me everything. How could I have been so stupid? That's totally what it is!

There's a weird feeling in the pit of my stomach, and the thought of another bite of anything suddenly makes me feel as if I'm going to vomit.

"You know, Dad, I'm not feeling so good. I think I'm going to take a bath and head to bed early if that's okay."

Dad looks up, surprised.

"You sure? You want me to do something?" he asks.

"No, I'm sure. I'll be fine."

"You're not stressing about that audition anymore, are you?" And just like that, I'm pretty sure I'm going to lose my dinner. Just what I need, one more thing to tie my stomach up in knots.

I run to the bathroom but don't vomit. Instead, I take a long hot bath with lots of bubbles and turn on some music. By the time I get out, my hands and feet are so pruney that my fingerprints would be mistaken for raisin prints. It's only 8:30, but I wrap up in my robe and climb into bed, still feeling a little nauseous. I grab my phone from the bed stand and see missed texts from Violet and Mom. Instead of reading them, I send a group text to both of them.

ME: Not feeling so good.
Going to bed.
Love you.

Then I turn off my phone and fall asleep.

I wake up dry-heaving sometime during the night and barely make it to the bathroom. After vomiting, I stumble back into my room, turn my phone on, and look at the time—2:56 a.m. This isn't just nerves. Something is wrong. Dad comes in just as I'm climbing back into bed and tells me he's not feeling well, either. Great.

I spend the next unknown amount of time moving from the bathroom to my bedroom in a haze. I'm not sure if it's food poisoning or the flu. But I don't care either way. All I can do is fall back to sleep between trips to the bathroom. When I am awake, my head is hazy, and I can't seem to keep track of anything. The only thing I want to do is sleep.

Chapter Forty-Two

NOT SUNDAY!

When I finally emerge back into the land of the living, I fumble with my phone in the waning darkness, only to realize I've missed two entire days. It was Thursday when I was eating dinner with Dad and stressing about the audition that was due in two days, but now my phone clearly says Sunday, 6:17 a.m. Sunday. I squint at my calendar in the growing dawn. Sunday? How can it possibly be Sunday already? Not Sunday!

Yesterday was the application deadline. I ignore the 12 new messages on my phone, turn it back off, and groan as I pull the pillow over my head and hope to go back to sleep. I don't. Tears surprise me as they roll down my cheeks and moisten my pillow. I wanted it so bad, but apparently not badly enough to get over my stage fright. Now, even if, for some reason, they would take a day-late audition, there was no way I'd be able to record an audition when I can hardly muster the strength to hold my phone up, let alone play a piano piece. I cry for a few minutes, but my body must still be exhausted from fighting whatever bug this is, and I fall back to sleep. I wake up next to Dad, sitting on the edge of my bed, stroking the hair away from my face,

"Hey, El."

"Hey," I croak in response, my voice raw and sore from disuse.

"That was a doozy, wasn't it?" I try to pull myself up to sitting and do feel a little better.

"How do *you* feel?" I ask him.

"Okay. I don't think I got it quite as bad as you." Dad lifts a soup bowl I hadn't noticed before from my bed stand.

"Think you can eat?"

"I don't know, but I'm starving," I tell him.

"Mrs. Silva brought over some chicken noodle soup."

"How'd she know we were sick?"

"When neither of us answered our phones, Mom called her and asked her to check up on us. I was awake enough to answer the door, and she told me I looked terrible and to leave the door unlocked and go back to bed," Dad laughs softly. "I guess maybe we aren't as good at taking care of ourselves as we thought we were."

Dad stays in my room and chats with me as I finish the soup and begin to gain my strength back.

"I think I need a shower," I tell him. "I smell terrible, like vomit."

"You kind of do," Dad says with a smile.

Chapter Forty-Three
THIS IS WHO I AM

I try to put thoughts of the summer music academy out of my mind. Try not to think about the incredible line-up of teachers and mentors. Try not to think of weekends with Violet and Ethan. Try not to be sad that I missed out on something that could have been really, really incredible for my life. Try not to think how that was my chance. My one chance to practically secure my place in a college music program. And I blew it. Blew it because of food poisoning, or, if I'm being honest, I blew it because of my ridiculous fear of performance and my inability to overcome it. I try to put it all out of my mind, but it's hard to do.

When I get out of the shower, I pull on comfy sweats and climb back into my bed with my hair wrapped up in a towel. Dad must be showering now because I hear the water running from his bathroom. I turn on my phone and send off a quick text to Mom and Violet.

ME:	I'm alive! Feeling better. That was rough. Will call later when I have more strength.

Both of them must be worried because they both respond within seconds with messages of relief and love.

Then I open the eight texts from Dean, which is weird since I just saw him a few days ago.

DEAN:	Hey
DEAN:	Hello?
DEAN:	Are you ignoring me?
DEAN:	Are you mad at me?
DEAN:	Please don't be mad
DEAN:	Elody, I'm sorry, it wasn't my place, but I couldn't let you pass this up. Not after my birthday present.
DEAN:	Please respond
DEAN:	I'm sorry.

What in the world is he talking about? Does he think he got me sick, and I'm mad about it? Because I'm pretty sure this was food poisoning from the leftovers we'd been eating, and he had nothing to do with that. What would I be mad about?

Before I can text him back to ask, my phone pings with all the emails coming in.

I scroll through the junk mail about car insurance

and a new skin procedure until one catches my eye, and I stop. I click on it, then I sit up straight in bed as the words swim in my head.

```
Application Complete. Thank you for submitting
your recorded audition. Our panel will be
reviewing your application and will be
making decisions by the end of next week.
```

Wait, what? Completed? I know I was practically unconscious, but there's no way I somehow recorded and submitted an audition while I was, what, asleep? There has to be some mistake.

"Dad?" I call out, but I can still hear the water running.

I go to my desk and open my laptop. Quickly, I type in the website and pull up my application. Sure enough, there is an uploaded file. A file named *Untitled 06_4*, which obviously means nothing to me. I stare at it without moving. How did this happen? Was I sleepwalking? I mean, sleep playing. Sleep recording. Sleep uploading! And if so, what random recording file did I actually upload? My hands begin to shake as I move my finger on the trackpad so the arrow hovers over the file.

One click. One click, and I could see just how humiliated I should be. Just then, Dad peeks into my room.

"How you doing?"

"Dad, did you upload a file for my application?"

"No," he says, confused but not concerned. "Oh, El, was yesterday the deadline? I'm so sorry, honey. Maybe you can email and explain; I can absolutely vouch for you that you were not in a position to be recording anything," he says.

"Uh, no, Dad, it's okay," I say, only half listening. If it wasn't Dad, then it must have been me. Me in a delusional state.

"I'm going to run to the store and get some apple juice, maybe some Sprite too. What sounds good to you? Anything?" he asks. I'm still staring at the file.

"Yeah, Sprite is good," I say, completely distracted.

Dad leaves, and I wiggle my finger on the trackpad again. I have to know, right? I have to click. I can't live the rest of my life wondering what random recording is floating around there in the universe. I mean, I could send them an apology email, tell them to please ignore my application, something, anything.

I close my eyes and click. The music starts immediately, and I recognize it. I open my eyes and blink twice, then stare at myself on the computer screen. The recording is a little wobbly at first. It's being taken from behind me and a little to my left. I'm sitting at my piano, and you can see my profile and my hands moving over the keys with a sureness that strikes me, even in this absurd situation. I'm playing "A Sky Full of Stars." I'm playing Dean's birthday song. And that's when his texts pop back into my head. I lift up my phone and re-read them.

Everything fits together now. Dean being quiet when the song was done, him looking over my shoulder as I logged into my profile, his mom saying he remembers everything, him having to leave to do his mysterious homework, and the texts. Without me realizing it, Dean recorded me playing his birthday song and then submitted it as my audition for my application! I don't know whether to laugh or cry. I'm partly horrified at the invasion of privacy and partly touched that he'd both think of it and go through with it. And strangely relieved that it was done and in, and I didn't even know about it.

The song ends, and I click on the file again. This time just listening. And you know what? Everyone was right. It is amazing. And even though I never turn to look at the camera or introduce the song, it displays what I'm capable of perfectly. I'll never be the performer someone else will be, but my talent is perfectly displayed. This is who I am, and this is what I'm capable of. If they want me in their program, they will know what they're getting.

Chapter Forty-Four
SO NOT OKAY

I don't think the conversation I need to have with Dean is one we should have over text, and even though I don't really know what I want to say to him, I need to see him. I slowly unwind my hair from the towel and brush it out. I'm surprised how even though I feel so much better, my body is still weak. Brushing my tangled hair feels like a monumental task, and I don't think running a marathon could leave me as exhausted as this. I have to rest after a couple of minutes. Finally, I text Dean.

ME: Hey. You busy?

He immediately responds.

DEAN: NO!
ME: Meet outside? Might still be contagious.

I think this is food poisoning, but you can never be too sure. By the time I make it down the hall, out the front door, and sit on the front porch, Dean is already coming across the yard. He stops when he gets close.

"Whoa, hey, what happened to you?"

"I'm not sure. Pretty sure it was food poisoning. All I know is I'm alive, and I'm glad whatever it was is over." Dean sits down cautiously on a step below me, keeping a little distance between us.

"You okay now?"

"I think so, just exhausted and really weak."

He side-glances at me, trying to figure out my reaction to what he did. When I don't say anything, he raises his eyebrows at me with questions shooting out of his eyes, and I nod.

"I know."

That's when he turns his whole body toward me with his face like a puppy dog that just finished eating your favorite shoe.

"I'm sorry, Elody, I'm really sorry. I shouldn't have sent it without asking you first. I just didn't want this opportunity to pass and for you not to apply. This would be so incredible, and I know you want to do it." He shakes his head in regret, and the slump of his shoulders tells me more than any words could ever explain. "I didn't record it planning to send it,

I promise. It's just when we read the requirements, I realized we already had a recording of exactly what they were asking for, and you wouldn't have to record one and be nervous, nothing else. It was already done!" I'm pretty sure he could keep going on for, oh, about forever, so I cut him off.

"Dean, I'm not mad. I mean, I probably should be, but honestly, I was so sick there's no way I could have sent something in, let alone record something. Now that it's done and it was turned in on time, I'm kind of relieved. You saved my chance at getting in."

He looks at me like he can't quite believe what I'm saying. But I know he hears me.

"Wait, you're not mad?" he questions.

"No."

Dean's face breaks into a grin that looks completely regret-free, so I need to clarify.

"I mean, again, I should be mad. It was totally an invasion of privacy, and so not okay, but I'm not mad."

He wipes the smile from his face and nods.

"Never, ever do something like that again."

"Oh, I won't. Trust me. I've spent the last two days tormented by your silence. I'm never recording anyone without permission again."

"Or logging on to someone else's account and uploading a video, pretending to be them." I raise my eyebrows and give him the look that my mom used to give me when she wanted me to say "thank you" without actually having to tell me to.

"Right, exactly. Never anything like that again," he says. We grin at each other and are quiet for a few minutes.

"Thank you, Dean. Thank you for caring about me that much." He nudges me with his arm, nearly knocking me over.

"Anytime, El."

Chapter Forty-Five
AT THIS TIME TOMORROW

The week goes by quickly, and each day, I feel a little bit better. With the audition in and acceptance emails not expected until Saturday, thoughts of Hoopcoming fill my head. Friday night, I'm getting ready for bed when my phone pings. I look over to see Zane's name, and my heart nearly stops. I've never gotten a text from him before, but I did save his number when he called a couple of weeks ago.

ZANE: Still good for 7:30?

For a moment, I try to imagine what he'd do if I said no, but instead start replying.

ME: Can't.

And then, I accidentally hit send before I realize I

only wrote one word. Frantically, I start typing again.

ME: Wait

Three dots are already blinking on the screen.

ZANE: Like, you want me to wait for something, or you can't go anymore?

ME: Sorry, I meant "CAN'T WAIT!"

Three dots blink, then disappear, and I feel like I might pass out while waiting for his response. Then, they appear again until finally, his message pops up.

ZANE: Gotcha. Cool. See you tomorrow.

I flop onto my bed and pull a pillow over my face. Are you kidding me? I can't even reply to a text properly, and now, at this time tomorrow, I'll be on a date, having to actually carry on a conversation.

Chapter Forty-Six

LIGHT HALOS BEHIND HIS HEAD

Although I've been missing Mom, I do enjoy how quiet the house is as I get ready for Hoopcoming. I'm on my hands and knees digging under my bed for the small wrist purse that used to be Violet's that she gave me that will match my dress perfectly when, instead, I pull out my love poem notebook. I've been so preoccupied with other things the last couple of weeks I haven't even opened it. I pause in my wrist purse search to flip through it. Wow. I have spent an incredible number of days writing about the boy I'm about to go to Hoopcoming with. This has kind of been my dream for years, but it feels a little less . . . less of something, I'm not quite sure what. Just then, my phone rings, and before long, Violet is on a video call, instructing me on every move I make as I finish getting ready, minus the wrist purse. She has called multiple times in the last few days, ready to give advice on how my hair should be, which perfume to use, and how much mascara I should wear. Now, I'm looking in the mirror, struggling with my hair.

"El, twist it a little more before you push the pin in," Violet tells me. I've kind of had enough, so I pretend to bump the phone and hit end. I love her, but enough is enough. Zane hasn't even rang the doorbell, and my stomach is tied in a knot so big it would take an entire basketball team to untangle it. I keep trying to breathe deep and do all the things Mom always talks about to fight my nerves, but none of it really seems to be helping. Violet calls back, and I respond with a text telling her that I love her and need to leave just as Dad peeks his head in the doorway.

"You all right? Need anything?" he asks.

"I got it," I tell him, trying to calm the jitters in my voice. "Just finishing up my hair, then I'm ready." I push one last hairpin into the twist of hair at the back of my head and turn to look at the half-up hairdo that Violet and I decided on. I close my eyes for a second, enjoying a moment of quiet before Zane arrives.

"Okay," I say, taking another deep breath and standing up. I turn to Dad, and a smile spreads across his face. He nods his head, and I can see he's trying not to cry. "What do you think?" I ask.

"You're beautiful, El Belle." I smile in response

and smooth the front of my dress with my nervous hands. Despite my confusion, my nerves, and the general fluster I usually feel in a situation like this, I do love the reflection of my perfect dress in the mirror. I glance from the mirror to Dad and give him a smile.

"You're always beautiful, though, you know that, right?" Dad continues. I step to the doorway and give him a hug, knowing it may mess up my hair but not caring.

"Thank you, Dad." And I kind of feel like maybe I'm ready. I sit back down on the edge of my bed and buckle the way-too-high shoes on my feet just as the doorbell rings. Dad and I make eye contact, and he raises his eyebrows.

"You ready for this?" I nod because, ready or not, that's all I can do.

Dad and I answer the door together. Zane is standing on the porch in a navy blue suit with sneakers so white it looks like he cleaned them with a toothbrush. His hair is damp as if he just showered right before throwing on the suit and automatically looking amazing, unlike the hours I spent in my room. The sun is setting, and when he turns toward me, the light halos behind his head. He smiles his dazzling, crooked smile at me, and every other thought I've ever had in my head suddenly evaporates like water on a hot summer sidewalk.

"Hey, El Lody, you ready?" I nod, still too stunned to speak, and turn to Dad with probably a look of panic in my eyes. He nods to me with a small smile as if to say, "You got this," and I step out onto the porch.

"Oh, a picture," Dad says. Zane and I awkwardly turn so we are facing the sun, and I'm not quite sure how to pose. Violet and Mom talked so much about these pictures, but they never actually said how I was supposed to pose in them. Finally, after a moment of awkward nothing, Zane loops an arm around my shoulder, and Dad says, "Smile." We do, he takes the picture, and we're off, and I'm suddenly grateful that Mom got called to work unexpectedly. If she had been here taking pictures, this would have turned into a full-blown photo shoot.

"Wait," Zane says just as we finish. "I'm supposed to give you this." He pulls a wrist corsage from his pocket and hands it to me. It's a little crumpled, and one of the petals is falling off, but it's still beautiful. Light blue carnations with little green buds around them. I slip it onto my wrist and hold it up closer so I can see it.

With a little panic, I wonder if I was supposed to get a boutonnière for him. Violet didn't say anything about getting one, but maybe Mom was planning to help me with that, and in her rush to leave, she forgot. Oh well.

"Thank you," I say, smiling up at him sheepishly. It comes out a little raspy, and I realize this is the first thing I've said to him since I opened the door. I clear my throat, "It's beautiful." I look back over my shoulder at Dad as we walk down the driveway toward Zane's brother's car. Dad gives me a thumbs up, but I don't return it as I quickly move my attention back to not tripping. Zane opens the door for me, and I climb into the back seat. As I sit there, my heart begins to thud so hard I think it will burst the seatbelt off of me. What am I doing? How am I going to survive an entire date? But when Zane gets in, he smiles at me again, introduces me to his brother and his date, and then starts talking. It's not like when Dean talks and talks and talks, but I can see he's trying, and when he asks me questions, they kind of sound as if they're coming from a list he made. I answer them and then try to ask him the same questions. This is a tip Violet gave me while we were talking this morning, and it kind of works for the entire ride to dinner.

Chapter Forty-Seven

SLIGHTLY MORE AWKWARD

When we arrive at the Italian restaurant, I get out of the car before Zane can get around to open my door. I'm not sure why, but it suddenly feels more awkward to have him open it for me. He comes to my side of the car just as I'm shutting the door.

"Okay," he says. I have no idea why, but I can hardly look at him in the eyes. I wish Violet was here. She'd know exactly what to do and say. I take a deep breath, trying to envision Violet. *That's* it. I need to channel my inner Violet. For some reason, this strikes me as really funny . . . picturing the search for a bunch of tiny Violets deep inside of me, and a giggle sneaks out.

"What?" Zane asks, and my face flushes. I didn't mean to laugh out loud.

"Oh, nothing," and now I feel bad. I hope he doesn't think I was laughing at him. We follow Zane's brother and his date as we enter the restaurant silently to find a small group waiting for us. I don't know any of them, but one girl looks familiar. Zane introduces me to all of them, and the familiar-looking girl with a pink stripe in her hair says, "Hey! I think we were in first grade together!"

"Huh, cool." Is it cool? I don't know. I scramble in my brain, trying to remember her name from first grade or five minutes ago; either would be just fine, but I come up with nothing. "Remind me of your name." I know Zane just introduced them all, but trying to hear and remember six names all at once isn't something I regularly practice.

"It's Olivia, but you can call me Liv," she says with a toss of her pink-streaked hair.

For a minute, I hope that if I can be seated next to her, maybe this dinner won't be as awkward as I anticipate. I'm relieved when I'm seated toward the end of the table with Zane on one side and another boy across from me. This is Zane's good friend, apparently, because they have an awful lot to talk to each other about. Liv is on the other side of me, but I quickly realize she might not have been the best table mate because as soon as our orders are placed, she is very much consumed by her date—hanging on to every word he says.

Even though Zane is very involved in the

conversations around the table, every once in a while, he pauses and asks if I'm okay, which I appreciate, but makes it slightly more awkward since he seems worried about me. My stomach is in knots. I'd like to blame the food poisoning from a couple of weeks ago, but let's be honest: those butterflies have completely taken over. So even though I like fettuccini alfredo, I mostly just keep moving it around my plate, hoping it looks like I've eaten more than I have, and feel a huge relief when the tiny chocolate mints are finally brought to the table, and we can leave.

Zane's brother turns up the music as soon as we get back into the car, so it's hard to have a conversation. Zane looks over and smiles at me, and I smile back, trying to look as if I'm content and relaxed and just enjoying the drive from the restaurant to the high school.

I feel even more nervous when we pull into the school parking lot. Since I started homeschooling in middle school, I haven't been inside the high school since Violet graduated. My palms are sweaty, and I try to dry them on my dress, hoping it doesn't leave any marks. We're quiet as we begin walking in, and then Zane says, " Oh, piano, right? You play the piano?" As if he was trying to remember what other topics were on his list of things to talk to me about. I suddenly feel bad, as if maybe I should have made a list, too, but I can't think of a single topic to bring up.

"Yeah, I play the piano," I say, and my mind immediately drifts to the application. Any day now. I need to get in. If I want a future in music, I need to get in. The website said two weeks and two weeks was yesterday. Any day, I'll know.

I'm so consumed by thoughts of the summer music academy, the application, and remembering the audition that I don't even realize that we haven't said another word to each other the entire walk to the school. Maybe that's the key to not being nervous . . . thinking about something that makes you even more nervous than the situation you're currently in.

Chapter Forty-Eight

A TINY WASTE OF MY, WELL, LIFE

Just before we get to the door, I reach out and stop Zane. Somehow, the necessity of my question sends thoughts of the application to the back of my mind. My needing to know is bigger than my fear of reaching out to touch his arm.

"Zane, wait," I say. He pulls his hand back from where it is, reaching for the door, and turns to me in surprise.

"'Sup?" He asks, glancing in confusion at my hand still on his arm.

I take a deep breath. I need to know. I don't know why I need to know, but there's a niggling in the back of my head that won't leave me alone.

"Did Dean tell you to ask me out to Hoopcoming?" My voice is so quiet that I wonder for a minute if he even heard me since he doesn't reply. Instead, he looks over my shoulder as if he's trying to remember.

"Uh, so I was telling him . . . there was this . . . kind of?" He says it like a question like he's asking me. But how am I supposed to know? That's why I'm asking him.

"So, he did?" I ask again.

"He just told me he didn't think you'd say no."

"Huh."

The niggling in the back of my head seems to be nudging me now, but I'm not sure I can handle the answers. "Did you want to ask me?"

"Sure, I mean, you're cool and all." He gives me the half smile that I've been gazing at in the yearbook for the last hundred weeks, and for some reason, my stomach doesn't even do a backbend, let alone a flip. There's nothing. I mean, of course, he's gorgeous. You'd have to be blind not to think that, but all of the days of wondering how it would be to have him even talk to me suddenly seem like maybe a tiny waste of my, well, life. And you know what? It's kind of okay. I smile at him.

"You're cool, too," I say. He just looks at me, shrugs, and reaches for the door handle. Apparently, it's not as cool a thing to say as it was in my mind. But, oh well.

Chapter Forty-Nine
NEARLY KISSING HIM IN THE PROCESS

Hoopcoming is held in the school gym, but for the money they must have spent to disguise this place, they might as well have rented out the White House. We walk in and stop; for a minute, I'm overwhelmed and need to take it all in. It looks nothing like a school gym. There are so many balloons above us I can't even see the ceiling. They are lower than the ceiling, too; I can't quite figure out how they did that, but it gives the whole giant room a kind of cozy feel. The walls are covered in draping fabric, making the room seem like we're literally in the clouds. Except instead of angels playing harps, we have music so loud that even in my fancy heels, I have to stand on tiptoe and lean close to Zane to hear anything he says.

Immediately, Zane is surrounded by friends as if they've been waiting for him to arrive. Someone steps on my dress, nearly making me trip. I yank it up and lean down to inspect it. There's a small tear near the edge, and my heart sinks—we've been in here maybe two minutes, and my dress is already scarred. As I stand back up, someone bumps into me, and I step sideways quickly, nearly losing my balance. When I finally right myself, I realize there are at least five people between me and Zane. How did that happen? I go up on my tiptoes to see if I can catch Zane's eye, but he doesn't seem fazed by the group around him.

I look around for Dean but don't see him anywhere. For the last two weeks, I've been trying to get him to tell me who he is taking without any success. Tonight, I should find out, and for some reason, that has caused the butterflies in my stomach to dance way more than thoughts of being next to Zane. I don't understand. This . . . being on a *date* with Zane . . . is what I've been wanting for so long.

I suddenly feel panicky. I hardly know anyone, and I am in a large group surrounded by people, but I basically feel totally alone. I want to act like I fit in here, but every cell in my body is telling me to flee like Cinderella at midnight. I try to pull out of the crowd, my spot quickly filling with someone more eager to get in on the action.

"Hey, fancy meeting you here." The voice is very close to my ear—obviously, it'd have to be for me to hear it. I turn, nearly kissing him in the process, which makes me blush instantly.

Dean. I feel a giggle of relief start to rise.

"Hey! You're here!"

"Yeah, I told you I was coming," he smiles and raises his eyebrows.

"Oh, I meant more like, RIGHT here," I yell back at him, tiptoeing up to his ear. One of the people moving into the group that surrounds Zane, and by default, *me*, bumps into me again, and I start to fall. A long dress, heels, and too many people are not a good combination for a girl who struggles to stay on her feet in normal situations. Dean reaches out and takes my arm, steadying me. He leads me off to the side, slightly out of the group, and I feel a sigh of relief escape me.

"You okay?" he asks, then looks around. "Where's Zane?"

"You see this crowd right here? He's the nucleus," I say, pointing over my shoulder.

"Right, and you're out of that because . . ."

"Well, I didn't mean to. I just kind of got lost out of it," I say, trying to make sense of it in my head.

"Wait, where's your date?" I ask, looking around as if she was standing next to us, and I just hadn't noticed.

"There you are!" Zane interrupts us, taking my other arm. "Sorry, lost you there for a minute." I didn't tell him it was more like five, nor that I kind of wanted to get lost, but whatever. He doesn't even seem to notice the frustration on my face. "This is great," he says, taking it all in, and I try to let my irritation go.

"Yeah, it's cool."

"Let's go dance," he says, pulling me toward the dance floor. I turn back to Dean.

"See ya!"

Zane notices Dean for the first time. "Oh, hey, man!" he calls over his shoulder as we walk away. It's as if Zane is in his own kingdom, surrounded by his subjects. He pulls me to the center of the dance floor back into the nucleus with him, and panic suddenly makes my heart pound. Zane seems so comfortable out here moving around, shaking his head, and I feel like I'm going to die. I look at everyone around me, none of whom are looking at me; instead, everyone seems to be in their own worlds. I bounce my knees a little bit, careful not to move my feet too much. What was I thinking? Why did I let Violet talk me into wearing these heels?

I bend my arms and try to move a little to the beat of the music. I mean, I get music, at least there's that. Zane says something that faintly sounds like a "yeah!" But to be honest, I can't hear him at all; then he moves closer to me. My heart begins to pound harder, but it isn't the kind of pounding that I expected. There's no swoon. Instead, I almost feel panicky. Someone else steps on my dress, and I feel it pull. I really liked this dress. Zane is watching me, so I smile up at him—I mean, I try to smile, it might look more like a grimace, who knows—and keep bouncing to the music. The song changes, and with a tidal wave of relief, I watch the crowd thin as a slow song starts. Zane reaches out to take my hand and tries to do a spin before moving into a dance position. Once again, between the train and the heels, the whole thing is more of a clockwise shuffle. I can't make eye contact with Zane—I can't do it. I'm sure he's danced with a hundred girls more graceful than me, and at that moment, I just don't have it in me to see that in his eyes. Instead, I put my hands up on his shoulders and look around the dance floor as we gently sway side to side.

All the other couples are close to each other, arms wrapped around each other's necks and backs. I feel Zane tug me a little closer, but I stand my swaying ground and feel a blush rise up my face. My mind is a whirl. I do not understand this. I think about the many times I've imagined holding hands with Zane, watching movies with his arm around me, even kissing him, and that stupid, stupid dream. And now, here he is, *dancing* with me to Ed Sheeran, with his arms pulling me tighter, and all I want to do is run (well, more like hobble) away. I take a deep breath . . . maybe, I'm just nervous, you know, my first dance, really first date too. I take a deep breath and look up at him and smile. I try to make it a real smile, but Zane isn't even looking at me. He's looking at a girl three couples away who is wrapped in the arms of a guy I remember from elementary school. Even back then, all that kid ever talked about was football. I don't know the girl, but it only takes me a minute to recognize the look on Zane's face. It's the same look I've seen in my own mirror for a hundred weeks. Smitten.

Suddenly, the strangest thing happens. My heart is filled with a feeling I didn't expect tonight. I know, with the way he can't stop looking at her, you'd think I'd be green with envy, wishing I was that girl, or more wishing that Zane was looking at me like that, but that's not it—not it at all. All I feel is empathy. I know exactly what it feels like to have a crush on someone for a long time, and the truth is—I'm starting to feel like that long time is coming to a close.

"Hey," I say, pulling Zane's attention from the girl. "Want to tell me about her?"

And then the most amazing thing happens. HE BLUSHES. Yep! Despite the dark lights, I'm close enough that I can see an obvious color spread across his face.

"Who?" he asks, trying to keep from glancing at her.

"Her, over there," I say, nodding my head toward her. "It's okay. Start with her name," I say with a genuine smile.

"Really? You don't mind?"

"Not at all." And I really don't. We spend the next two songs with his mouth close to my ear, but instead of whispering sweet nothings, he tells me all about the queen of his crush castle. And I get it. And I don't say a word besides "uh-huh, uh-huh" because I'm good at that.

That's when I realize that all this time I'd dreamed of and imagined him, I didn't have a crush on him, really. I had a crush on the imaginary boy that lived in my head but wore his face. Zane was a living, breathing, dancing boy who had a crush on a girl that was very different from me, and that was okay; in fact, that was good. Zane was polite, kind, and cool, and I'm pretty sure I've already made it clear, very attractive. But we don't really know each other, have nothing in common (unless you count this unrequited love situation we are both familiar with), and honestly, we don't have that much fun together. It doesn't mean there's anything wrong with him or anything wrong with me. It just means that, well, he's no longer the king of my crush castle.

CHAPTER FIFTY

FACE-SPLITTING GRIN

I'm standing by the punch table next to Zane, who is actually turned away talking to his friends, including his crush queen and football boy. I'm in a gorgeous dress, with a perfect hair-do (thanks to Violet's video call rescue session) in shoes that are very uncomfortable, at Hoopcoming . . . everything I ever dreamed of; yet, it feels kind of anticlimactic, and now that my crush on Zane seems to have all but disappeared, all I can think about is . . . Dean.

I'm starting to feel a little awkward again. I mean, being okay with Zane's crush or not, I'm still standing here practically by myself, and for a minute, the comfort of my kitty cat pajamas flash through my head. Then I hear the DJ talking and try to listen. All I can make out is "request" and "greatest hen." "Greatest hen?" Why is he talking about a hen? Wait, that doesn't make sense. Then it starts. Oh, "Greatest friend." Coldplay's "A Sky Full of Stars" begins playing, and at that moment, I know. I just know. I feel almost panicky as I look around until I spot him. He's standing across the room near the DJ, all casual and cool with a smile as big as Texas, watching me. I can't help myself. I smile back. He walks over and puts a hand out without even saying anything. I take his hand and then glance back to Zane, who is all smiles. He nods a tiny nod of understanding to me, and I nod back.

Dean leads me onto the dance floor, and he puts his hands in the actual dance position. I can't stop smiling, even with the shuffle I'm trying to do. This is supposed to be perfect, but suddenly, Dean stops and gets down on his knee. Okay, this is weird. Is he going to, like, propose? I mean, I kind of *just* realized that I might actually *like* him. Violet got married young, but 13 is REALLY young. I mean, long engagements are a thing, but . . .

"Lift your foot up," he says. Oh, right. I get it now. I lift my foot up, holding on to Dean's shoulder as I balance on one foot. He takes my ridiculous shoe off and tosses it to the edge of the room, then we switch, and he takes the other one. He stands back up, and I wiggle my toes in relief. Ahhh. So much better. He takes my hand again and places the other on the small of my back, and then we dance. Like, really dance. I mean, I had no idea Dean could dance, and actually, I didn't really know I could dance either, but here we are spinning around the dance floor like he's Derek Hough, and we're on "Celebrity Dance-off." And it's *amazing*. I just pretty much let him lead (okay, sometimes lift or drag) me around the floor, both of us smiling like little kids in a candy store, and when the song ends, he pulls me into a hug, and it's pretty much perfect, like the most perfect moment of my life.

Then a fast song comes on, and before you know it, we are jumping with our hands in the air, and I'm hitting into all sorts of people, and maybe some of them are just as clumsy as I am. The strobe lights are flashing on and off, and like flashes from a movie in fast forward, I see Zane near us, his face in a huge grin; the girl he's crushing on is near him, whipping her hair around. I see other people that look familiar, and I see Dean. He's yelling out the words to a song I don't know and jumping so hard he's looking a little sweaty; when he catches my eye, he smiles. His face breaks into that face-splitting grin, and there's a feeling inside of me I've never felt before. A feeling—if I'm being honest—better than a swoon. He moves closer to me, grabs my hand, and tugs me into a jump with him. Laughter bubbles inside of me. I have no idea what the words are, but I start yelling anyway, and it's surprisingly, well, better than anything I could have imagined.

Chapter Fifty-One

MAYBE IT ISN'T ZANE

"*I don't get it.*" I'm talking to Violet on speakerphone, still wrapped in the warmth of my bed. I don't even know what time it is, but I woke up to Violet's call. She wanted all the details of last night.

"Don't get what?" she asks.

"I liked him for so long, and now it's just over."

"Maybe it isn't Zane that you really liked," she says.

"What do you mean? I've liked him for like a hundred weeks!"

"Yeah, but you didn't really even know him. Do you think you actually liked maybe just the idea of him more than actually liking, you know, him?" I think back to my "aha" moment on the dance floor and the realization I had about Zane then.

"Yeah, you're right." I think about that for a moment. "It's just weird, you know? Like, now what?"

She laughs.

"Okay, on to bigger and better, I guess. Like Dean." I can hear the slyness in her voice.

"Violet!"

"Oh, come on, how are we still talking about Zane when Dean pulled one of the most romantic scenes of all time? Like, *Say Anything*, *Ten Things I Hate About You*, and *The Fault in Our Stars*, all rolled into one, and maybe better." Violet went through this phase in high school where she rated all teenage romantic movies going back into the '80s. I was really too young for romance at the time and lost interest pretty quickly; then again, I think of my love poem notebook. Maybe it really did affect me more than I thought.

"So," she says, changing the subject. "Any response from the music academy yet?"

"I haven't even checked!" I'd gotten so consumed with Hoopcoming and then analyzing everything about Hoopcoming that I hadn't even checked my email since before I'd left for the dance. I roll over on my bed and pull open my email on my phone.

"Well?" Violet asks. She has no patience.

"It's still loading," I tell her. Then my breath catches because there really is an email from them. I sit up.

"Oh, my gosh, Violet, there's an email!"

"What's it say? What's it say?" she's nearly

screaming. I have to move the phone even further away so she doesn't burst my eardrum, and I read the email out loud to her.

```
Dear Elody,
Thank you for your application and audition submission. Our panel of instructors and musicians has reviewed and discussed your piece, and we are happy to offer you a spot in our summer music academy.
```

I can hear Violet screaming and yelling to tell Ethan. I flip back to the video call, and the camera is a blur of her jumping up and down. Even though what she's doing is exactly how I feel inside, I just smile, the biggest smile I've ever smiled . . . and I can't stop smiling. I don't stop smiling when I run into Dad's room to tell him or when I call Mom to tell her. I don't stop smiling when I pull a hoodie over my pajamas and walk across the yard to Dean's house.

Chapter Fifty-Two
NEVER FELT SO GOOD

When Dean's mom opens the door, she's obviously a little surprised to see me.

"Hey! Aren't you up a little early after last night?" she says, ushering me in.

"Yeah. Violet called and woke me up, wanting to hear a full report."

"Ah, yes. I can see her loving every detail," she says with a smile. The house smells like cinnamon and something sweet baking. She leads me to the kitchen. The smell reminds me of life when Violet still lived at home and a wave of something that feels like homesickness washes over me; I suddenly miss her so much.

"So, I'm assuming you are looking for Dean?" she says, putting a pot-mitt on her hand and pulling something from the oven. I nod in response, even though she isn't looking and doesn't really need an answer from me. I thought it smelled good before, but now the smell is even more intense, and my stomach grumbles in response.

"Every Sunday when I was growing up, we made German pancakes. I'm not as diligent as my mom was, but we try to carry on the tradition." The baking dish is filled with a beautiful golden-brown, fluffy masterpiece.

"Tell you what —I'll go wake him up if you cut up these strawberries."

"Okay, thanks," I tell her, taking the knife from her and moving to the cutting board.

I slice the strawberries and am once again reminded of Violet. I loved helping her in the kitchen, not that I really helped much, but I'd sit at the bar and cut stuff up while she cooked and talked to me, telling me everything about her day. Kind of how Dean does. I look up to see Dean following his mom down the hall. He, too, has a hoodie on but with basketball shorts. His hair is a wild mess, standing on its ends, and his eyes are puffy with sleep, but his smile is wider than the Grand Canyon.

"Hello," I say. I'm sure my smile is reflected back, just as wide. I put the knife down and move around the corner.

"Hey," he says, climbing onto the bar stool.

"I have something I wanted to show you," I tell

him, handing him my phone with the email open on it. He takes it and blinks a few times, trying to focus his sleepy eyes. I try to keep my face straight and my mouth shut while he reads it, but it's so hard! Giggles of excitement bubble up, and it's all I can do to keep them from bursting out.

"Wait, what?" Dean tosses the phone onto the counter as he jumps up and grabs me in the biggest hug I've ever had, spinning me around as we both laugh.

"You did it!" he says, setting me back down and looking me square in the eyes.

"No, WE did it," I tell him, and I mean it. "I wouldn't have done it without you, Dean. Thank you." He's still holding on to me, and as he leans closer, I hear Dean's mom clear her throat. A major blush rushes over me, giving away exactly what was in my mind.

"Congratulations, Elody! That's such great news," she says, putting two plates with German pancakes on the countertop in front of us.

"Thanks, Mrs. Evans." I glance over at Dean, and his face-splitting Grand Canyon smile is back on, and I can't help having my own. Then we dig in and stuff ourselves full of German pancakes drenched in syrup with strawberries, and life has never felt so good.

Chapter Fifty-Three

ALWAYS BE MY EL BELLE

By the time I leave, Dean has convinced me to come back in a couple of hours (he's kindly allowed me to go home and shower and get dressed for the day) to practice shooting hoops. Okay, I'll be honest; there really aren't going to be any hoops. Really, I'm going to practice catching a pass when he throws it to me without shrieking in terror and collapsing into a fetal position.

I walk home across the yard, feeling too full to move quickly. I think about how nice it would be if maybe Zane stopped by to play, too. There are no butterflies in my stomach thinking about him; instead, I just think it might be kind of fun. Who knows, maybe we could even invite the queen of his crush castle, too, and actually play a game. Wait, who am I kidding?

When I walk inside, Dad's sitting on the couch

and looks up from the book he's reading. He smiles at me.

"Hey, El Belle. Did you tell Dean?"

I can't help the smile that fills my face. I think it might be permanent at this point.

"Yeah, he was pretty excited." Dad pats the couch next to him, and I sit down, nuzzling in next to him into that place under his shoulder where I fit so perfectly.

"And how do you feel?" he asks.

"I'm pretty excited too . . . and a little nervous." Dad leans his head down so his cheek is resting on my head. I think of Dad, Mom, Violet and Ethan, Dean, all these people—my people—who care about me and have been cheering me on, and my heart feels about as full as my stomach.

"Oh, you'll be amazing. You're always amazing." He pauses a minute, "And if not, they'll just send you back home to me."

"Dad!" I laugh and teasingly pretend to pull away from him. He's laughing, too, then he gets serious.

"No, I know they'll love you, but I'll sure miss you, El Belle."

"I'll miss you, too, Dad, but no matter what, I'll always be your little girl."

"That's right," he says, wrapping his other arm around me in a hug. "You'll always be my El Belle."

Author's Note

When I was young, I was very, very shy. As shy as Elody. In fact, when Elody tells about playing the piano and shaking so badly she hit every other note than what was on the music page, that came from my own life. I found a lot of comfort in reading. I could meet all sorts of people and have all sorts of experiences without actually having to talk to anyone. That's why I was very young when I knew I wanted to become an author. I wanted to write books like the ones I fell in love with as a small girl. When I was 11, I began writing to an author I admired, and he wrote back. We were pen pals for a few years while I was going through some really hard things. I will forever be grateful for that author, who not only wrote books I could escape in but also took the time to befriend and encourage a young aspiring author. I learned that there are people in the world who have never even met you that still care about you. Reader: I care about you.

Elody's best friend, Dean, is named after this author. Thank you, Author, for writing to a young girl.

Molly has been writing stories since she learned to read them. She was born in upstate New York and has lived in two countries and six U.S. states. She earned her BA in English at Brigham Young University. She loves reading, writing, traveling, painting pictures, being outside, and exploring new places with her favorite people. She also loves adventures like jumping out of airplanes over the ocean, riding camels in the Sahara, and even swimming with sharks in the Pacific. Molly is the author of several books for young people. She currently lives in Arizona with her husband, three incredible kids, one spoiled puppy, and never enough books.

**Want more insightful, empowering, fun children's books?
Want activities and links to go along with the story?**
Visit us at lawleypublishing.com

For updates and info on New Releases follow us at

lawleypublishing   @kidsbookswithheart

Printed in the USA
CPSIA information can be obtained
at www.ICGtesting.com
LVHW020814091024
793283LV00003B/22